JOSH

IVAN SOUTHALL

FRONT STREET
Asheville, North Carolina

First Front Street paperback edition, 2005

First published by Angus and Robertson (Publishers)
Pty. Ltd. in Australia in 1971

Library of Congress catalog card number: 75-187795

FRONT STREET
A Division of Boyds Mills Press, Inc.
A Highlights Company

To "Aunt Clara"
in fond recall.
With a little twist here and a bigger twist
there
a story grew.
Kith and kin, take no offence; they are
not you.

CONTENTS

SATURDAY

1

The train, a motor-driven carriage of one compartment looking like a large motor-bus, stopped with a jolt at Ryan Creek at about ten minutes past eight. Sunlight had gone, twilight was short, and all the things that Josh had hoped to see—even though he was uncommonly tired and nervous—were lost in the dusk. Things like the old Plowman homestead on the hill and the "famous" railway bridge built of logs long ago.

A fellow travelled for most of the day, stood round for hours waiting for the connection, got stiff and sore and dull and hungry, and still the dark beat him into Ryan Creek by minutes. He knew when he crossed the famous bridge because he heard the clatter and felt the sway, but he had wanted the thrill of seeing. Dad had said, "One of these days the train won't make it. One of these days it'll go clean off the edge, and then the Plowmans will look sick." Perhaps Dad had not meant it.

The train should have been in at seven fifty-three, but time of arrival at Ryan Creek seemed to be so unimportant that it stopped five times in the last seven miles to put people down or pick them up—with not a railway station in sight. Or were there seven stops in five miles? Josh, rather irritably, lost count.

At one point, leaning on an elbow, the driver yarned about a cricket match with an odd-looking character who neither boarded the train nor got off. He happened to be there, milking a cow, like something in a disordered dream. There he sat like a giant frog on a box, with a black-and-white cow and a tin bucket *inside* the railway fence. So the driver stopped. Perhaps he stopped there every day. Perhaps in winter they yarned about football and on the 31st December reviewed the events of the year. Josh didn't know, he had never travelled that way—which must have made him the only stranger on the train, and the only Plowman, apart from his sister, not to have done so before.

Up and down the length of the compartment the passengers called to each other with familiarity, to say the least of it, using the most startling language. They were a rugged lot. Some of their adjectives were so raw that Josh didn't know where to look. Honest, the things they came out with were enough to curl a fellow's hair. Even that terrific-looking girl of about fourteen or fifteen could turn a colourful phrase.

One young man who might have had too much to drink—it was a Saturday night after all—called to her, "Hey, Betsy. Come over here and gimme a kiss." He wasn't nasty or difficult or anything really unpleasant, just noisy.

"I wouldn't kiss you," she shrilled back at him, "if every other monkey in the world was dead." Everybody howled with laughter and the young man giggled and swayed his head and gleefully thumped his knee several times.

Someone else yelled, "How's your old man, Betsy? Is he still doin' time?"

"That's one thing he's never done, Snowy Jones. He's not one of your mob. My dad keeps his nose clean."

"Does he just? You don't know the half of it, Betsy girl, the thievin' old cow."

"You hold your tongue, Snowy Jones, or I'll be letting your family know about you."

They were revelling in it and perhaps so was she. There was a cheeky grin on her face at times and then the men seemed to like her more, seemed to jostle for the right words to make her turn their way. Looking at that girl was a pleasure of a kind Josh had not known before.

"Pictures tonight, Betsy?" asked another old fellow who must have been sixty if he was a day, with two broken teeth and a greasy hat and a happy smile. "Sittin' in the back row with me?"

"When pigs fly, Pat O'Halloran, you crummy old man. You wouldn't be so cheeky if your missus was around."

Hoots of laughter again, good humour flowing free, even if the way they went about it made Josh uncomfortable at times. Thinking things like that was one matter, hearing them said aloud was another. But her voice, Betsy's voice, was such a disappointment. She looked terrific; hair with red lights in it, eyes with a sparkle, and clothes that gave her a boyish style. The sort of girl whose hand you wanted to hold and then go running together, running a mile. Twice he caught her eye, twice he caught himself thinking, "There must be a ventriloquist on the train. That horrible voice couldn't be hers."

Were they Ryan Creek people? They must have been heading for some other place along the line. Dad always said that Ryan Creek was as dead as a doornail, where people woke up once a week to go to church on Sunday. They got to church, he said, and promptly fell asleep again. If *these* people got into a church there'd be a riot. For all that, every member of the Plowman family, aunts, uncles and cousins, spoke of Ryan Creek with awe or affection. Aunt Clara lived there. "You've *never* been to see Aunt Clara, Josh? You've never eaten her egg-and-bacon pie? You've never played aeroplanes on her organ? You've never sat in her bath? Until you see Aunt Clara, Josh, gee, you haven't lived."

"Mum," he had nagged, for about the fourth year running, "what about it *this* summer? Can I go?"

"It's a long way, Josh. She can be very strange."

"Gosh, Mum."

"You won't be able to run home."

"Well, all my cousins have been. I'm the only one who hasn't. I *ought* to go. If those kids can stand up to her why can't I? If she died or anything before I got there she'd never forgive me. Dad's been. *He* went when he was fourteen. He went lots of times."

So the train stopped and he was there! And that noisy crowd, or most of it, went piling out onto the platform before his eyes, surprising him, even that terrific-looking girl.

Could that straight and ancient lady be Aunt Clara, the one the men touched their hats to, the one the girl almost curtsied to? That old lady could have been cut with care from a photograph taken fifty years ago. Everything out there had the same old look, faintly disturbing him. Old-fashioned picket fence along the platform glimpsed in the gloom, pale light-globes and old-fashioned poles, ornamental scallops sawn round the station buildings, everything looking quaint as if time had slipped a cog.

Of course it was Aunt Clara. There couldn't be two in the world like her. She had the Plowman look, as if the railway station belonged to her, as if the earth had been made by her. Fixing him with the Plowman stare, raising a finger to remind him that the rail car would carry him on if he didn't move. The passengers off were already gone. Unloaded parcels and crates mounted outside. She had peered at him and instantly known. He had thought his looks favoured his mother's side, had never realized before he could be picked so easily for a Plowman, too.

The finger was beckoning. "Hurry along, boy," it said, "don't sit there like a fool. That's not the Plowman way."

2

The weight of his bag dragged him to the platform with a thud, buckling him, and a hand was touching his shoulder resting there. "Stand up straight, Joshua. Let me look at you."

Josh was trembling, all confidence suddenly flown. The wobble had set in hours ago as soon as Mum and Dad melted into nothing and were gone. Meeting with Aunt Clara's approval was being a proper Plowman, as every member of the family knew. Being a proper Plowman was critical, like having a head, even if Josh reckoned the idea was mad.

When the Plowman cousins said, "Until you see Aunt Clara you haven't lived," they really meant, "You're nothing, Josh; until you do you're not alive."

Talk about fuss and family. Mum said it gave her a pain. "Who do the Plowmans think they are?" But she didn't address the question to Dad. "Take them away from Ryan Creek and they're nobodies, and not one of them has lived there in years. Only her. And what's Ryan Creek but the end of the world? With all respect to the people there."

Aunt Clara's hand was calling on him to rise like the touch of a sovereign's sword and getting up to face it was like raising a weight from the ground. Small. She was so small. He had to look down. Eyes down there, faint but huge behind spectacle lenses that must have been tinted, probably blue.

"You're tall for your age, Joshua. My word. We'll have to fatten you up, won't we?" Meaning he was a weed. Stretching his way and kissing him, catching him by surprise, a wet, cold kiss smelling strongly of tea. "You're a nice-looking boy. Your father was a handsome lad. He broke a heart or two. How are they all?"

"Very well, thank you."

"Your voice has broken! Oh, what a shame. That lovely boy soprano I've been waiting to hear. Have you left him at home? I hope your poems are in your bag and you've not left *them* behind?"

Josh with the prickles, trying not to sigh. "I've got them, Aunt Clara, they're here." But not for her eyes unless he personally turned each page!

"Come along then. Is your ticket handy? Give it to me. Pick up your bag. Don't leave it there."

He had no intention of leaving it anywhere.

Walking away from the pale light-globes along an avenue of trees, through a tunnel rustling with wind and all but obliterating the sky, except for the afterglow. Her touch still on his arm, in a possessive way, preventing him from changing his bag from side to side. Josh not thinking well, with noises in his head and nerves in his hands and already on the raw. Getting treated like a child!

"Your sister is six now. I'm still waiting for photographs. Will you remind your mother, again, please. Nothing I say has any effect and a letter each Christmas doesn't go far. You must have a camera in the house. Your father was camera-mad when he was here last time."

Does it matter, Aunt Clara? But not out loud so she could hear. What do you need pictures for? See one Plowman and you've seen them all.

"Come along, Joshua, lift your feet. You're scraping the leather off your soles."

The name is *Josh*, if you don't mind. Don't call me that word. But again not brave enough to say it aloud. And the bag was dragging on him, dragging him down. On to a long wooden footbridge, planks laid crosswise, unevenly worn, made for stumbling on when you were tired and the light was bad, gravel at the end of it, an uphill grade, propelled by Aunt Clara's commanding hand. Like being a horse with a bullock's load.

Far away at the top of the hill—extraordinary how far it seemed—one baleful street light marked the end of the road. You'll die, Josh, before you make it and then how far will you have to go? Yellow windows up there on the face of the hill flickering behind trees—who lived inside? A powerful smell of cows, Aunt Clara talking all the time, Josh trying to grunt with intelligent sounds. Cows everywhere, the place smelling like a barn, giving him shudders he could not explain, sweating flanks and hot breath imagined on warm night air, sloppy-looking mouths chewing gobs of cud and eyes as baleful as the street-light glow. Kids yelling somewhere, sounding so little they should have been in bed, and garbled song from the happy young man off the train, weaving up the hill towards the light-pole. Aunt Clara sounding sad, "A nice boy, too, I taught him for years, I'm sorry you're seeing him this way. Every Saturday night it's the same."

I've seen drunks, Aunt Clara, lots of times. … But the thought shot away unsaid, shot out through the top of his head, and Josh went slipping, went thudding down, with Aunt Clara crying aloud, "Have you sat in it, you silly boy?"

Josh wailing, "I don't know."

"Goodness me, what's wrong with you? Didn't you see it there?"

"Of course I didn't see it. It's *dark*, Aunt Clara." Josh pulling himself up, almost scared to touch himself with his hands. "Blooming cows! What are they doing out here messing up the road?" Hobbling to the verge and dragging his shoes through the grass making shuddering sounds.

"Is it on your clothes?"

"No, no, no." A sobbing sort of no.

"I'd have had to hose you down."

"Well, you won't have to, Aunt Clara."

"Your night vision is *very* poor. Carrots for you. I can see and I'm seventy-three. Never walk about this place with your head in the air. Cows live here."

Josh snarling, "Well why don't they put them in paddocks like other people do?"

"At this time of the year? The paddocks are bare. The only grass left is along the roads. Come along, that'll do, that'll do. Don't fuss so. Pick up your bag. Come along here. It's shorter this way."

Plunging into unlit dark grass, knee-high and crackling, like wading through paper, groping miserably, nose twitching for cows, eyes straining for them.

"Don't stumble! Walk ahead of me, boy. Can't you see there's a track? Bless me, your sight is bad. You must be undernourished. What does your mother feed you on?"

"*Food.*"

"And that covers a multitude of crimes! Why are you walking like that? Are you lame? Is one leg shorter than the other?"

"It's the bag! It's *heavy.*"

"Shouldn't be. Not for a boy of your size. The Plowmans are perfect physical specimens, every one of them. Have you outgrown your strength? Malt and cod-liver oil for you. I should have known when they told me you wrote poetry. Unnatural activity for a boy. Do you play sport?"

"Yes, Aunt Clara, of course I do!"

"Manly sports?"

"Yes, Aunt Clara! Running and cricket! You name it!"

"Cricket? Ah … that's what I wanted to hear. Football, too?"

"When it's *winter*, Aunt Clara, I don't play it now."

"Swimming?"

"Yes and no."

"That's not an answer. I expect more from you."

Josh grumbling to himself. "I get cold. I don't like the cold. I break out in goose-pimples all over. I sink."

"Doesn't surprise me at all. You're as thin as a stick. Ribs sticking out all over, no doubt. Skin and bone. Clotted cream for you. An undernourished Plowman. Goodness me. What's wrong with your father? Can't he earn the money to feed you? Does he spend it on motor-cars? Everything in the house on time payment? Refrigerators and all that rubbish? What about your teeth? Full of cavities, I suppose. All patched and plugged."

"I've got good teeth!"

"We'll see. Lots of milk and cheese for you."

"*I'm only here for a week, Aunt Clara.*"

"And that's the pity of it, but we'll send you home with an appetite they'll have to feed. Up here, Joshua. There's the gate. See it there. Good heavens, boy, *there.*"

When they got to it, it was only a strand of wire.

3

A light-bulb left burning over the back door, scores of moths and thousands of insects feverishly assaulting it, a broad veranda with a bluestone floor, cane chairs and wooden benches, veranda posts burdened with roses, bloated stag ferns heavy with sap flopping on the wall, an enormous white cat on the mat too bone-lazy to move, reluctantly shrinking as the screen door opened across it, reaching out a claw, allowing itself to be stepped over. Josh feeling like wiping his feet on it, feeling like snarling, "Shift, will ya, y'great fat thing."

Inside. Smells of flowers and wood smoke and old furniture and wax polish and pastry. Heavy shadows bulging with mysteries. Fibrous curtains, extraordinary things, rustling on long strings in arches. Dark doors shut with ruby glass knobs. Ceilings about twelve feet up. Black floors shining at the edges of straw mats. Josh dropping the bag with a thud. Pains of relief like arrows on fire bursting from his shoulders.

As if he had stepped into a museum after hours, as if he should not have been there, as if someone had his centuries topsy-turvy. Great-grandfather Plowman, whiskers and sideburns, watch-chain and all, darkly looking down from the wall. Darkly and disapprovingly as if someone had waved a smell under his nose. The original Plowman stare. Dad had said there were paintings of him everywhere. Self-portraits painted with an admiring hand. Spent half his lifetime studying mirrors.

"You can't leave your things there. Come along to your room."

Josh dragging the monstrous bag away from Great-grandfather's glare, staggering after Aunt Clara through the archway, strings and fibres chafing and rustling, catching in his hair, Aunt Clara ahead of him vanishing somewhere in a midnight gloom, fiddling with switches on the wall. Josh staggering into a cavern fourteen feet high and twenty feet square, heavy with lavender, lit with a strange red glow. Bead curtains stirring on windows, crystal leaves tinkling in the ceiling, gilt bedstead shining with knobs and swirls and satins, large enough to accommodate half a dozen full-grown Plowmans simultaneously. Great-grandfather, too. Great-grandfather over the marble fireplace, larger than life, adorned like King Henry VIII in regalia.

Josh groaning about God, not under his breath as he meant to, and allowing his bag to fall.

Aunt Clara beside him stretching upwards, up and up like an outraged church steeple. "Joshua, you will not take the name of the Lord in vain. In this house or anywhere within my hearing."

Now he was alone, yet from somewhere she called, "You'll find water in the jug. Don't slosh it around. Clean your teeth and brush your hair. Then we'll see about dinner."

In the middle of the cavern, drooping like a lost soul, kicking at his bag, and groping to the washstand, a huge marble slab mounted on a table, huge bowl with blue flowers painted on it, huge jug with a handle big enough to poke his head through, and a slab of red soap smelling like the stuff they put in public lavatories. Getting a hand on the jug, using both hands in panic, but it was like lifting a body and he was terrified of spilling it. Stupid idea. Stupid. Stupid. Everything was stupid everywhere. Why had he come? Hadn't Mum tried? "No, Josh, I'd rather you didn't. You're different from your cousins. She's an old lady and can be very peculiar." Mum should have bound him hand and foot and tied him to the doorpost.

The bed was so near … he turned and flopped towards it, but its edge was so hard and its mattress so high that he only half made it.

Was a hand fondling his hair?

"Joshua, don't go to sleep so soon, so early, it's only ten minutes to nine. …"

Was it imagination? So far away. Much too far away to care.

SUNDAY

4

A jug with blue flowers on it, huge, enormous, started forming round the fringes of Josh's consciousness, line by line, getting larger and larger and more unlikely. Curves and knobs and unfamiliar oddities started marshalling in the shadows, lining up for foot-drill. Great-grandfather Plowman dressed in absurdities wavering in the air like the King of Diamonds played from a pack too big to believe in. Music in the heavens like the sound of spheres, tinkling, tinkling. Leaves of crystal, dozens of them, scores of them, shivering like dragonflies trapped in spider webs, revolving, revolving, touching and tinkling. Higher, higher, red and awful, spilling out its threads, holding up its crystals, the last chandelier that ever should have happened. Higher yet, miles beyond it, roses on the ceiling, blooms and stalks and thorns in embossed pink plaster.

Josh shrinking into himself, cowed by majesty, wounded by purples and reds and pinks and icky-looking yellows and by pieces of furniture that simply had to be malevolent. What a place to have slept in. What a place to wake up in. Gosh, Josh, it's a miracle you're still breathing.

Struggling to a sitting position, sinking deeper into feathers, feeling horribly full but horribly empty, offended by vulgar bubblings lodged in his middle. Josh, you might need the bathroom. Where is it? You have an errand of some urgency.

Groping over the edge through acres of eiderdown that maddeningly slid along with him, groping with his feet for the floor, frantically, unbelievingly, no floor there, falling into a pit, collapsing on his knees smothered in satins. Is it a bed or a scaffold? Point to be decided.

Panting and pawing at the eiderdown and reeling from the room to the passage, striking a dull shoulder against the partly open door, shocking himself to a stop, grunting explosively.

Leaning there, back to the wall, aching and dejected, the urgency knocked out of him for the moment.

Oh, what a mess he had made of everything. What an arrival. At last there comes a Plowman who's a fool without trying, one who writes poetry (unnatural activity) and gets goose-pimples in cold water. The one she has to feed on cod-liver oil and carrots. The imperfect specimen who falls over everything and goes to bed at night as if dressed for a journey.

Oh yes, Josh Plowman, as if dressed for a journey.

Mum, it's set in already!

Feeling for his tie; she'd taken it. Checking his shoes; they were gone. Peering round the corner into the room; his bag had been put away. Strike me, Mum, when things go wrong I'm bound to be in it.

Night had gone too. Maybe half the day. Sunshine outside, streaming into the passage through leadlights around the front door, horrible-looking things, blue and green and blood-red sunlight pooling on the floor, looking like something that ought to be mopped up and sterilized.

Fully clothed in bed. How do you do it, Josh? No trouble at all. No dinner either. She'd probably been cooking it all day. He'd hit the bed and out he'd gone.

Lying there like a log at play, poor old girl heaving him around, unbuttoning his shirt and unknotting his tie, unlacing his filthy shoes. Glad you stopped there, Aunt Clara, for you and for me. A man's got his pride. If you'd taken off me pants we'd have had a word or two. I'd be chasing you round the block with your chandelier. And where did you put the bag? Neatly away? Unopened? It had better be.

Where's your bathroom, Aunt Clara? You've got one, I suppose. Which door? Mum's got a label on hers. *This is it*. Very handy. Saves a lot of time when visitors call.

All doors shut and all looking the same. That's the trouble, Aunt Clara. Open the wrong one and I'll have you leaping out of bed.

A doorknob in his hand, glowing ruby-red, turning it silently and peeping in through a crack about three inches, wide. Huge room inside. A table long enough for ten fat Plowmans, armchairs for as many, three portraits of Great-grandfather, no more time for looking. Wrong time of day.

Tiptoeing on, waddling, through the horrid chafing curtains in the archway, coming into the lobby near the back door. There stands Aunt Clara. White bonnet on the side of her head, *purple* dressing-gown reaching the floor, hanging onto a cup of milky white tea big enough to water the horses.

"Good morning, Joshua."

What a get-up. This year's fashion for witches and warlocks.

"I won't need to teach you how to sleep. You have an excellent way of your own."

Josh producing a sick grin. Incapable of producing anything else just then.

"It's half past eight, my boy. You've been asleep for twelve whole hours."

Josh staring at the cup of tea, dismayed.

"Yes, Joshua, it's for you. A nice hot cup of tea. I was hoping it might wake you up. But come on into the kitchen and join me there."

All of it, Aunt Clara, *all* that tea.

"You're an odd one, Joshua. Not much to say. Don't you drink at all? Come on into the kitchen and sit yourself down."

"Please, Aunt Clara. ... It's the bathroom I want, not a cup of tea." Almost weeping aloud.

"At this hour of the morning? Bless me, you don't want a bath now. Gather the sticks? Stoke up the heater? Run the water? It'd take an hour. Wash in your room, boy. Everything you need is there."

"It's *not*, Aunt Clara. Not everything I had in mind."

"Oh, *that*. It's under the bed. Where did you think it would be?"

Gosh, Josh. ... "I can't use one of those things, Aunt Clara." Wailing at her. "I just couldn't."

"Why can't you? Something wrong with you?"

"*Please*, Aunt Clara. ... I want to go to the *bathroom*."

"If you mean the Throne Room, Joshua, it's outside. Places like that *we* do not keep indoors. Follow the brick path, it'll take you there, and watch where you put your feet. The fowls are out for their morning stroll."

Trying so hard to get there with a little dignity, trying to pull the remnants of his manhood together, but at the instant he put his foot outside the doormat squashed into shrieking fragments of cat. Josh screaming and fleeing in panic, Aunt Clara's voice pursuing, "Bless me, are you blind? Broad daylight! A white cat as big as a Dalmatian! George, poor old George. Come to Auntie, you poor old thing."

5

"Joshua!" She was at the bedroom door, knocking. "May I come in?"

"No."

Pause.

"Why not, Joshua?"

"I haven't any clothes on."

"*None* at all?"

"I'm washing myself, Aunt Clara."

"Bless me. What an extraordinary boy. Would I need to remind you to wash behind the ears?"

"No, Aunt Clara. You would not."

"You didn't come back for your cup of tea."

"I'm sorry. But I don't take milk in my tea."

"It's gone quite cold."

"I said I'm sorry."

"It was your loss, lad, not mine. But I am perplexed. When did you have a meal last?"

"Yesterday at lunchtime."

"And you're not hungry yet? You're not thirsty?"

"I didn't say that, Aunt Clara." His voice much more of a little boy's than he wished.

"All right, finish your wash and dress for Sunday-school. Your clothes are hanging in the wardrobe, or hadn't you noticed? Your suit and black shoes, and please, not the tie you wore yesterday. Whose taste is it? Yours or your mother's? It flabbergasts me."

Footsteps going away.

Hurling the towel at the wall and wanting to break things. Sunday-school! All the Plowmans were the same; organize the hide off you. Suit and black shoes on a holiday! And he had *nagged* Mum into it. It was why Mum didn't exchange letters or send photographs, why she didn't make a fuss of the old girl like all the others, all the other Plowmans crawling on their hands and knees. "I married him," Mum said of Dad, "for himself. Not for his aunt's money."

So his ties flabbergasted her. Did they? When the colours in her house were *horrible*!

Suit hanging in the wardrobe? You could say that with knobs on. Everything in the wardrobe. Everything emptied out of his bag when he'd wanted her not to touch it. Nothing left in it. Upside-down empty.

Josh! You've been standing here washing and not thinking of it. Where's your book of poetry? The bally bag's empty. Josh, she asked you about it. She asked you at the station. Would she have taken it without your permission? Which she'd never have got in a lifetime!

Ploughing into the wardrobe throwing things everywhere. Not a sign of it. Dragging drawers open, every one of them sprinkled with lavender. His singlets crackling with lavender. He'd be perfumed like a poppy! Singlets hurled at the floor. What had she done with his poetry? Every drawer open and slammed shut again. Round the shelves, up and down the mantelpiece, underneath the bed, in and out of horrible lumps of furniture, behind the curtains and under the carpet, stirring up dust until he was coughing. Getting frantic. Turning paler. Finally feeling sick and quite desperate.

She had it.

Josh, surrounded by disorder, trying to control himself.

Mum. ... What's she done to me?

Mum, she's taken a liberty you'd never dream of.

Josh buckling where he stood, sitting in a huddle, wrapping his arms across his shoulders, swaying, trying not to think of that old lady reading his poetry. Reading things that not even Mum knew were written, things he might have shown her later when he felt braver. Poems that weren't finished where he'd said things stupid and still wasn't sure whether he ought to keep them. Dreams written down to remember, things he never talked about. Poems about impatience, about waiting to grow older, strange feelings that weren't meant for old ladies. Others so juvenile they should have been torn out long ago. Josh, why did you bring it? You should have left it at home for Mum to look after. She wouldn't have pried, she'd never have opened it. "Your mind and emotions belong to you, dear." That was Mum's reasoning. "When you share them with me I take it as an honour. I don't expect it. And when you keep them to yourself, that's your business, that's your life, your private compartment. I have things, too, I don't want to share with anybody."

Dad was different. Doubting Dad made Josh embarrassed, but you had to face reality. He had a way of giving Josh a very odd expression. "Why look at me like that, Dad?" "You're my son, aren't you? Why not?" Was it the Plowman way of thinking? Mum came at everything from other directions. Doubting Dad was why he had brought his book with him. Thinking Dad might go hunting for it out of curiosity, as he might have done already on other occasions.

I'm ashamed, Dad. It's awful. But the risk was there and I couldn't take it.

Was it Aunt Clara's way of thinking also? Because he was her nephew she saw it as her right to take without permission? To plug in a wire and listen to his thoughts any time she wanted to. Like the keyhole-God Mum told him not to believe in, the one distorted out of shape by people who must have been unhealthy, the spying God who remembered bad things and added up the failures. "People who love each other," Mum said, "don't spy on each other, and God is loving."

Aunt Clara, you wouldn't take it any further, would you? You wouldn't be peeping through the keyhole. You must have heard me throwing stuff round the bedroom. You must have wondered what I was doing.

Josh leaping for the door and throwing it open, but the passage was empty.

6

House smelling of bacon frying, Josh so terribly empty, hungrier than a hunter, but making his way with great reluctance to the kitchen. Like setting out on a journey that had to end a bad way, knowing the future before it happened. Trying to face her eye-to-eye, knowing she had read things. How could he do it? Trying to speak with a voice that wouldn't break with passion. Trying not to start the row that would have to hurt everybody, Mum suffering because of it, Dad finding life even harder in the family because he'd always been the only Plowman out of step with the others. Gosh, Mum, what a thing to happen and I've still got a week of it. Sitting here with her, living out a week of it.

Aunt Clara glancing up from the stove sighting him briefly over her shoulder, Josh troubled by her spectacles, two glazed circles glinting like huge eyes that in an instant might see the world and remember everything in it.

"Your place is under the window, Joshua."

Blue smoke layered in the kitchen, drifting in the light as if nothing had been moving to disturb it, as if Aunt Clara had been standing there thinking things over. Thinking what things over? Smoke—like a witch's kitchen—all in undulating layers flecked with dust particles, drifting, as if it might not be prudent to break through it.

"You look nice in your suit."

Josh not expecting that kind of comment, but not surprised by it. He had known her glance had not missed much of anything.

"Handsome."

Josh grimacing with annoyance and plunging into the smoke half-expecting it to have substance that might resist him. The old seat under the window all of a wobble, its long cushion slipping as he edged along it, the window-sill exactly of the height to bear hardest on his backbone.

"You wear clothes well, Joshua. The thin ones often do. I hope you like Bran-Bits. You'll find them there."

Breathing heavily. Trying to cope. Drawing away from the window-sill rubbing at him. "I don't know what Bran-Bits are."

"Pour some cream on them and a teaspoon of honey. We don't use sugar here."

"We don't at home either." Defiantly. "I like things bitter."

"Do you? That could be why you're thin. Put the honey on. You need it."

Breathing even more heavily, struggling to say nothing, irritated because she wouldn't look at him, because it was her back she presented to him, and because the pan over the fire was spitting too furiously; the wrong kind of sound for someone who feared that each word was hastening the blow-up that must not happen.

"Say your grace, Joshua. We haven't eaten a meal in this house for half a century without asking God's blessing on it."

"You've taken my poems! That's spying!"

Josh stiff and sore with fright, horrified because it had happened, wanting to call it back, but at the same time wanting to fight it to a screaming finish. Expecting her to swing on him, to come back at him with a voice as passionate as his own. But she didn't. "It was not my intention to spy, Joshua. That's not a kind word. You need not say your grace aloud, but say it, please."

"What have you done with my poems?" Still shouting at her.

"I have read them. Other than that I have done nothing with them. Now say your grace and eat your Bran-Bits. Your eggs are ready."

Struggling. Struggling. Tempted to crash his fists on the table, to set the crockery and the cutlery dancing. Fighting it down.

Bless O Lord this food so it doesn't choke me dead Amen.

Hating himself because he was starving; despising himself because he ate the stuff like a rebellious infant sternly reprimanded. Selling out for a plate of lousy Bran-Bits. *Be Regular. Be Healthy.* Picture on the packet of a champion footballer who wouldn't have eaten Bran-Bits if he'd been dying from hunger. But with a couple of sandwiches and two bottles of lemonade since yesterday's breakfast! Flesh and blood had limits. Spooning the horrible stuff into his mouth, crunching at it like gravel.

Yesterday's breakfast! How many thousand years ago was it? Everyone quiet except Caroline, Caroline chattering like a sparrow. But you couldn't tell a six-year-old to leave her chattering until later. Not Caroline.

No wonder Dad had been edgy. He must have known what was coming. He'd been through it often. But Dad was loyal and never said anything against Aunt Clara. Mum didn't have to be loyal; she had not been a Plowman until she had married. Dad must have been sitting there sweating, weighing up his doubts against his hopes that Aunt Clara wouldn't play the tyrant.

Was this why all the Plowman cousins were full of bravado? Were they all cracking hardy to each other? Each scared to admit to anybody that stopping with Aunt Clara was deadly. All making sure that Josh got his ration of misery along with the rest of them.

That old witch over her cauldron, fat spitting, purple gown drooping by the hem to the hearth, ash dusted on the bottom of it, ash and flour fluff and cat hair. It was like waking up in the Dark

Ages. That old witch reading his poems. That old witch reading things that not even Mum knew were written.

Coming towards him, bringing hot plates, sitting opposite murmuring, her head bowing over one rasher of bacon and one egg, rubbing in the insult, making his own serving huge but her own almost invisible. Would she dare ask a blessing? Her eyes coming up to him, Josh refusing point-blank to meet them, trying not to swallow his food whole, trying to make out he didn't care whether he ate or left it. Nearly choking on it, with a hole inside him bigger than the rest of him. Wolfing it. Trying to look the table over for afters without looking. Not a slice of toast, no bread, no marmalade, nothing, only a huge glass of milk that he refused to recognize as part of the menu.

Breakfast in a museum listening to the prize exhibit eating.

Everything else as quiet as a graveyard with clocks ticking. No traffic sounds. No sounds of people. Trying to squint sideways along the window but getting a crick in his neck. Nothing out there except a cow with full udders moaning for someone to bring her a bucket.

"You haven't drunk your milk."

Catching him by surprise. Catching his eye when he had vowed she wouldn't. There she sat dabbing at her lips with a serviette.

"I don't like milk." Meaning to make a statement of it, but hearing it come out sullenly, because full-face, in good light, she wasn't what he had expected. Looking so old and pale and different from faces at home across the table; not looking hard or angry or stern or anything like that; simply like a nice old lady, which wasn't right, which didn't fit.

"It's time you learnt to like milk. It will please me if you drink it.

"You didn't think about pleasing me when you took my book."

"Joshua. ... We're not going to discuss it."

"We are!"

"We're not. It's Sunday morning and I'll not have Sunday morning disturbed by argument. But I will say this; I didn't spy. That was cruel of you. That hurt. If I had wished you not to know I had seen your poems wouldn't I have returned them while you were asleep? Think about that. Now kindly clear the table and stack the dishes in the sink. Then perhaps you'd better go to your room and put it straight. And make your bed while you're at it."

Away she went, her gown whispering over the floor, and he started swearing helplessly under his breath until he embarrassed himself.

7

Josh standing in the wide passage outside his bedroom door with his face feeling as long as his foot, waiting on Aunt Clara, listening to a frantic confusion of nervous clocks all ticking against each other, each clock scared it was going to stop and the others would get ahead, each wondering whether Aunt Clara had wound it up last night or last week or last year or whenever, swinging their pendulums, rotating their spheres, clicking their ratchets, stretching their springs, clanking their gears. Clocks everywhere and not one to be seen, only heard. Curtains rustling, lavender wafting, floor polish lying in wait to unfoot the unwary, wallpaper glinting with gilt and burnish, landscapes in oils brooding in the shadows, ghastly-looking sunlight bleeding through the stained-glass portals, Ryan Creek outside unseen and unexplored like a jungle inhabited by savages.

Aunt Clara emerging from her boudoir all done up like a dog's dinner. "Ready?"

"Yes, Aunt Clara." A lie if ever there was one.

Opening the front door to the sunken porch with garden steps waiting to be climbed to the street-level gateway. Like mounting a platform to be exposed to public ridicule. Kids of all kinds imagined lurking behind bushes, peering out of sunflowers, digging each other in the petals. "Here's another Plowman dolled up in his Sunday pretties. What a prune. What a poppy." They'd be there doing their sniggering. He knew all about country kids; they were as tough as old leather.

Fifteen steps he counted from the front door up to the High Street. A gate of brown pickets opening against the pressure of a screeching spring and shutting with a vicious clack. Aunt Clara and her bundle of worn religious books, the broad-brimmed black hat shading her face, holding firmly to his arm, maybe fearing he would escape, talking, "That's the O'Connor house beside the drapery shop. Good boys, Bill and Rex. They've been anxious for you to come. It was their sister on the train last night. The place with the shutters up was your Uncle Geoffrey's house."

Josh not caring about anything, only hearing her because he wasn't deaf. Striding up the High Street trying to look cheerful was like trying to laugh with a knife stuck in his back. As wide as a paddock, that street. Where were all the trees of the night? The ones that had flickered across the lights? Taken indoors, probably, for shelter from the sun. It was a hard-looking place, yellow and hot. No wonder they went by train on a Saturday to get drunk. The greater wonder was that they came back.

A small boy of about eight with red hair and masses of freckles striding on the other side of Aunt Clara, huge strides, huge grin, Aunt Clara's books mysteriously in his possession, chattering like a bird in the way that Caroline chattered, and breaking into a skip. Had he fallen from a nest? Voices coming from all directions. Kids erupting out of the earth. Suddenly under mass attack.

"Hullo, Miss Plowman."

"Hey, hey. Wait for us."

"Hey, there's Joshua. He's come, he's come. Ain't he tall?"

"I know my text, Miss Plowman. I can say it backwards this week."

"Miss Plowman, Miss Plowman, do you like my new hat?"

Kids swarming round all wanting to shake his hand, all reaching at once. A man twenty yards away leaning over a fence, giving a shout, "I'd heard he'd come. Fine big boy, Miss Plowman." Aunt Clara's hand on his shoulder giving it a particular squeeze that made him feel awful, absolutely awful. Josh all mixed up, not understanding her or himself noticing the flush mounting in her cheeks where the paleness had been. Somehow getting moving again, all of them together, little kids under his feet and others bigger than himself, not what he'd expected, nothing like it at all.

Was this the pattern for Sunday mornings, Aunt Clara in the midst of a mass of kids, getting pushed off her feet by affection? Little kids asking questions, questions, questions, older boys and girls hanging back at the fringes but giving grins of sympathy, warm grins, friendly grins, not sniggering, nothing of the kind; among them a heavy-bodied, heavy-lidded girl staring with disturbing frankness, as if staring were not in the least ill-mannered but the most natural thing in the world. Josh looking round vaguely for the girl on the train, the girl they'd called Betsy, and even *she* was there and the flesh of his hand started tingling because she might have touched him. Too late now to know for sure. Being carried along all the time in the middle of the crowd, not quite himself, not wholly there, confused and unsteady from noise and movement and words, trying not to stare at Betsy as the heavy-lidded girl was staring at him, getting carried along into a church hall where voices dropped in key and everyone whispered hoarsely as if talking aloud was not the proper thing to do.

"You're sitting with us."

The friendly push in his side coming from a burly fellow with close-cropped hair, not the sort Josh expected to find in Sunday-school. Not with Aunt Clara there. Was he about sixteen? Was his name Bill? Was he one of the O'Connors? Josh couldn't pick them any more; couldn't pick anyone except the girl on the train. "Bill," she was saying, "I've left my collection at home. Lend me threepence."

Bill giving her a scowl. "Where would I get threepence? I've only got my own."

"Who's got threepence?" Betsy holding out her hand, swinging it around. "Bill's being lousy; his usual style."

Josh digging down. "I have. Give us a second to find it."

But she didn't hear or made out she didn't and vanished, Josh losing track of her, Burly Bill guiding him through a swarm of ten-year-olds and bringing him to a corner where bench-seats were arranged in a square.

Josh flopping down, feeling breathless and hot and mauled, looking up into the eyes of the heavy-lidded girl on the other side of the square. She was leaning his way; she was smiling. "Are you only fourteen?"

Josh feeling a flutter of disquiet, feeling defenceless and exposed, trying not to hear.

"And you write poems?"

Josh going hot and cold, distrusting everything about her, and trying to avoid her by shuffling along the seat to make a space for others, but she crossed with a swoop and sat beside him as if he had made room for her.

"About flowers and butterflies?"

Shaking his head almost too vigorously, flinching from her weight at his side, going panicky. That awful Aunt Clara had been talking! She'd think she'd be impressing them, but they'd be killing themselves laughing. They'd be lining up now like vultures for picking and tearing, wearing one face for her and another for him. He'd known it was too friendly, he'd known they'd been pushing it too hard to be genuine.

"About sweethearts and things like that?"

She was not letting up and was pressing him close and scattering his senses, but someone was whispering at his other ear, tapping his shoulder. Three cheers for Bill O'Connor. "We're going shooting tomorrow out at Mitchell's. Do you want to be in it? We'd ask you for today if we could, but can't of course. We get rabbits mainly. Got a wallaby once, a little beauty."

A rugged-looking kid, looking bunched up with muscles, leant in from the side. "You asking him about tomorrow? What do you say, Joshua? Call you for about nine? Bring your lunch if you're coming.

Josh feeling nervous, wondering whether he was getting pressured from a new direction, never having held a gun except for potting at tin cans and missing, but grasping at the suggestion just the same and nodding, trying to ignore the heavy-lidded girl's persistent nudging, even thinking of asking, "Why not today? Why wait till tomorrow to go shooting? Let's go *now*." But Betsy was sliding into the seat next to the kid with muscles, spoiling Josh's concentration. Trying not to stare at her, trying to watch her round corners, but still getting nudged from the girl beside him. "Do you write poems about being in love?" She wouldn't be quiet and was much too close to be ignored without rudeness.

"I don't write about anything much." Sounding completely breathless. "I write them hardly ever."

"That's not what Miss Plowman says."

"Leave him alone, Laura." The muscle-bound kid started hissing with impatience. "Don't push him. She's always going on about poetry. Don't let her rile you."

"You mind your own business, Harry. I only want to know what he writes them about. I'm only being friendly. What's wrong with that?"

"You're bothering him, Laura."

"I'm doing nothing of the sort. Am I bothering you, Joshua? I'm not, am I? I'm making him feel at home. He's shy, aren't you, Joshua? I know what it's like to be the odd one out."

"For Pete's sake, sis, leave him alone! If he doesn't want to talk, he doesn't want to talk!"

Josh suspecting he was in the middle of a family argument that could have been going for days and that the last thought Laura might ever have had was a nasty one. Josh stammering, because everyone was embarrassed, "I'll tell you, Laura, I'll tell you, I'll tell you later." But her brother Harry seemed even more displeased; and then a chord struck on the piano and everyone stood up and faced the front, in a sudden quiet as disconcerting as the immediate response. Josh's heart was thudding and he felt uneasy and strange and conscious of Laura still leaning his way as if she had known him for years, not just for a minute or two, as if she had known him always but he had not known her. Josh wishing for Aunt Clara to be closer at hand, but all he could see of her was the crown of her hat, Aunt Clara striking the chord a second time. Everyone singing furiously, words he couldn't follow, words he didn't know. Something about timely happy and rising morn and beam celestial view. Making no sense to Josh and less to the rest of them he was sure. Singing roof-lifting furiously, never looking at a book, never guessing at the meaning of a word.

Josh shaking from head to foot in a strange world, scared of not knowing what to do. None of them would have believed that here was a Plowman who had not set foot in Sunday-school before.

8

Moving back down the street towards Aunt Clara's brown picket gate, Bill O'Connor beefing it along on one side, Harry Jones on the other walking like an ape, calling back and forth about traps set down on the creek each night ("Do you like a nice juicy rabbit, Joshua?"), about swimming in the dam and a cricket match on Tuesday against kids coming over from Croxley; "A real cocky bunch. Wouldn't we love to take them down a peg for a change. What are you like with the bat? If we can't play a Plowman in the team we can't play anyone." Laura was there almost breathing down his neck, Betsy he couldn't even glimpse, little kids had massed behind and in front, and the sun was very hot with dust lifting from the roadsides in gusts. Did the wind ever stop?

"Mr. Stockdale is preaching," Aunt Clara was saying as if announcing a major event. "He loves to see the young ones in the congregation. I hope some of you will be there to gladden his heart at three o'clock."

Josh's spirits sinking to greater and greater depths, knowing what that meant and Laura made it worse: "But he rambles on for so long, Miss Plowman. Last time he came he finished one sermon and started off on another."

"Laura!"

"Well, he did, Miss Plowman. I didn't think he was ever going to stop."

"None of us is perfect, my dear. We all have our faults. That we may not always share Mr. Stockdale's enthusiasm for length doesn't mean we cannot learn at his feet."

"I'd rather learn at your feet, Miss Plowman."

"Thank you, Laura, but you'll not be turning my head with flattery. Joshua and I will be there. Come along and fill our seat, and afterwards we shall have tea at my place. I believe there was an egg-and-bacon pie not eaten last night."

Her hand was on the gate but the kids hadn't gone. Their devotion puzzled and tired Josh. She didn't conduct Sunday-school by herself. Why didn't they trail the other teachers home? An hour and twenty minutes they'd been caged in that place. All that singing and praying and reciting of texts, all that stuff about God slaying tens of thousands of ancient Egyptians because they had worshipped someone else. What a God for a white-haired old lady to boast about. All the faces of all those kids, all their grins and smiles swarming about the gate, Josh praying for them to go, wondering whether they ever would, drooping in the middle of them from the sheer fatigue of trying to wear an acceptable front.

"Bye, Miss Plowman." "See you later, Joshua." "I'll try to get to church, Miss Plowman, though Dad was taking me out." "You got lots of parsley in that pie, Miss Plowman?" "Don't forget to bring your lunch, Joshua." "Yeh, we're taking him shooting, Miss Plowman, it's fixed, tomorrow of course. We'll practise cricket this afternoon instead." As if the shooting might have been arranged! As if the invitation might have been a put-up job!

In the house again, lavender and gilt and strangeness, standing beside her in the ghastly glow from the leadlights, his jaws sore and his head dull from holding a set grin for a length of time past all reason, and dreading the row that still had to come. Dreading it but waiting for it. Knowing it was now. Even Aunt Clara was looking suddenly strained.

"Come on through to the kitchen and we'll make a pot of tea. Won't take a moment. The kettle will be hot."

Trailing numbly after her into the gloom, his eyes bruised from the sun, not sure where to put his feet. Those horrible curtains again, rustling like reeds, chafing.

"Take off your suit coat if you wish. Sit out on the veranda, why don't you? I'll join you there. The wind will keep the flies away."

Stepping over the hissing white cat, somehow resisting an ill-tempered impulse to jump on it, throwing his coat over a chair back, wearily tugging loose his tie. Wind tossing the roses about, petals scudding to the wall of the house, the garden a feverish place of agitated plants, the sky hazed white, and Josh short of breath.

Oh, Josh. ...

All energy gone, everything emptying out of him, collapsing in the chair, even troubled by giddiness, the kind that could be relieved only by being sick.

Those kids must have reckoned he was stupid. Nothing stopping in his head long enough to take root. Grinning like a Cheshire cat all the time but not saying anything to them, not answering them, just grinning. Josh, they must reckon you've a screw loose. But they don't know anything about the Aunt Clara who goes spying in the night. Look, Aunt Clara, you can't go judging me like God for things I think. You don't know what other kids think. Do they ever tell you? You don't know what *anyone* thinks, because no one will tell you. That Egyptian story, God judging the wicked; aiming it at me; I'm not stupid. All the kids reckoned it wasn't in the lesson. They reckoned you were pointing it at someone. And you don't even know how the poems happened. Sometimes there *wasn't* any thought until the paper was in front of me waiting for words. But you think I'm rotten. ...

The screen door squealing against its ageing spring, Aunt Clara setting down a silver tray on an upended barrel, teapot of silver too, and cups of bone china so fragile he was scared they'd blow away.

"Bring up your chair, Joshua."

Watching that fat white cat stirring up his bones, stretching, and padding to her feet, winding himself round her ankles, purring, pushing, snivelling for the jug in her hand and getting what he crawled for, milk in his saucer. Aunt Clara should have shown him the point of her toe.

"Come on, Joshua, bring in your chair."

Josh dragging it across the bluestone slabs, wondering whether he ought to purr, suddenly being presented with a handful of china so thin his fingers felt like crushing machines. Balancing on the side of his chair, his trembling transmitted to the surface of his tea—milk in it of course—eating shortbread as dry as woodchips. No spit in his mouth. Talk about torment. She must have had those kids bluffed or paid them all by the week.

"Have you a Bible, Joshua?"

Josh groaning inside. *Bibles* she wanted to talk about. He should have known.

"I thought not. You couldn't find the psalm this morning. Laura Jones had to help you find your way through the books. You should have warned me, Joshua. A little preparation before we left could have saved much embarrassment.

Trying to swallow what seemed to be a mouthful of sawdust adhering to his teeth. Scared he was going to choke and drop the cup.

"I'll make you a present of the Authorized Version, I think. You'll have a feeling for its language and the intelligence to sort it out. I want you to learn your way around it and to read it as I read your poetry last night. Reach some decisions about it. Think."

Crumbs flecking Josh's lips, panting for breath, crumbs spraying right and left, Aunt Clara shrilling with shock, "Take a drink. Good heavens, boy, you'll choke."

Josh reeling to the edge of the veranda, somehow balancing his cup, and spitting the shortbread as far as he could spit. Drooping there as if he had been whipped, then trying to wash down the bits with tea that was scalding hot.

"Are you all right?"

Josh nodding in despair.

"Give me your cup before you drop it. You're a bundle of nerves. Do they ill-treat you at home or what?"

"No. ..."

"Are you sure you're all right?"

"Yes. ..."

"Do you want to sit down again?"

Josh slouching to his chair, avoiding her eyes, feeling dreadful stricken with humiliation for having spat.

"You're a bit of a riddle, aren't you? It's a very busy world you live in, but you've got it all inside. Those boys and girls of mine at Sunday-school; you must have noticed they're full of fun. No secret wells down too deep. Live on the surface, Joshua, out in the sun. They do. You're only young once and it's gone so soon."

Somehow he held on; somehow he had to think of Mum and Dad and the disgrace of answering back. They'd all get to hear of it; every Plowman this side of the black stump.

"Your poems tell me that, and if I look at you I see it again. Everything so intense. God didn't give us our emotions to turn our lives into a tightrope walk. What does your mother say when she reads poems like that?"

He couldn't speak to her, couldn't trust himself for the violence that was in him.

"Now why didn't you say to those boys you'd play cricket on Tuesday? They wanted to know. That's why they asked."

Longing to run away. Longing to get outside the range of her voice. Longing to be at home. But trying to tell himself that she wasn't being unkind, not meaning to be. Her voice wasn't angry. It was only the awful arrogance that all the Plowmans had; her surprise that anyone could think or act or be in any way different from her predetermined view. She couldn't help it; all the Plowmans were the same. He could never get along with any of them; there was always a row.

"Joshua, don't you hear me? Aren't you well? Are you sick?"

Looking up at her, knowing she knew everything about him there was to know. Knowing as much as God knew about the things that mattered to him deep down inside. Knowing she had no right to know. Looking up at her through his unmanly tears, lips forced shut on words he wanted to scream, violently throwing his chair aside and stumbling from the veranda into the garden not knowing what to do, stumbling into obstacles he couldn't clearly see.

"Joshua, come back."

"*My name's not Joshua. It's Josh.*"

Running away. Blundering down the garden trying to find the path, knowing he could never go back again in a thousand years. Running until a strand of wire struck at him under his ribs knocking him down, that ridiculous bit of wire she called her "gate." Rolling down a dusty slope through all sorts of filth, chickens and cows and every living creature that had passed that way, then limping through the crackling grass with a cluster of burrs as big as peas plucking at his kneecap.

"Joshua! Come back!"

"I'll not answer to that, not one more time." Whimpering to himself. "They did christen me, you know. They christened me Josh. We're not heathens, no we're not. Of course we've got a Bible, and we've got other books too. The Talmud and the Koran and all sorts of scriptures from China and India and everywhere else. We respect what other people think. That's what Mum says and it goes for me. We don't go prying or peeping or bullying or sneering if people are different from us."

Josh thought she was following, felt sure she was there, but when he looked back she was not to be seen.

9

He had come along here last night dragging his bag in the dark, a strip of dried-up grass, a road surveyed maybe when Adam was a pup, no earthly use for anything except cows and chickens and people on foot. Wind gusting in his face. Everything so breathlessly hot.

Flapping red hens squawking round his feet, stupid things flapping up the dust. Wire-enclosed paddocks below him as bare as brass, deeply scored with hoofs when rain had fallen last, a week ago or a month. Paling fences above him propped up with sticks. Rusty-looking outhouses built of kerosene tins beaten out flat. Fruit-trees up there tossing in the wind, gnarled old things pruned grotesquely out of shape. Cows on long chains out in front tethered to fence posts, three of the brutes, levelling the grass around them to yellow-grey arcs of earth, lowing at him as if they paid the rent. You move over, cows; you let me past. Weaving round their arcs, hair bristling on his neck, distrusting their horns, feeling their bleary-eyed stares in the small of his back.

Panting at the corner as if it were the edge of the earth suddenly encountered, pulling nervily at the burrs in the knee of his trousers, groaning for his clothes, for his best shirt and pants, all stained with muck and dust and looking as if they'd been worn for a month on an expedition to the interior. Brushing at himself with his hands, feebly, as if he didn't have the strength, and swearing from the futility of it. How was he going to backtrack? What could a fellow do when he'd burnt every bridge? Mum's voice sounding in his head: "Don't act so impulsively, dear. Do try to cultivate the habit of living a minute ahead."

Looking miserably along the grass strip past the old grey fences to Aunt Clara's at the end. If she'd followed at all she'd soon given up. If she'd called only once again, "Joshua, come back," there might have been a way out, but there wasn't any call and there wasn't any way back. Nothing but stupid cows and stupid red hens and heat and dust.

You've made your bed, Josh. You've got to lie in it.

You've burnt your bally bridges.

You've cooked your flipping goose.

Kids pouring down from the High Street corner, kids galore, cracking towels like whips, wearing them like capes, doing high-speed frolics as if school was just out.

Josh moaning out loud and hearing their cries against the wind.

"Hey. There's Joshua."

"Hi, Joshua. How's tricks?"

Trapped.

Wishing for a hole in the earth to sink out of sight. Betsy there, too. All the mob. The lot. They'd spot in a second that something was up.

"Hi, Joshua." Harry, the muscle-bound kid, Laura's brother. "What are you doing out in the street? You got influence or what?"

Laura looking like an acorn with a green bathing-cap. "Got your togs on? Coming for a dip?"

Kids breaking over him like a wave.

"Come on, Joshua. It'll cool you off."

"Yeh, we'll show you some water as good as anything you city kids have got."

"Gee, fella. Fancy her letting you out. That's great."

Overwhelming him as they had done in the High Street, almost carrying him off his feet, but that silly sick grin was back again and he couldn't wipe it off; all his thoughts getting scattered again; there was so much *noise*. The wave surging on again, Josh in the middle of it, resisting its pressure in a half-hearted way, feeling they were capturing him but not being sure, Laura possessing him from much too close, holding his arm, Burly Bill looming over him with a hand to his shoulder talking in his ear. "What have you been doing to yourself? You been in trouble? Where'd you cop all that dirt?"

Josh knowing it had to come; it was a wonder they had waited so long. "I tripped." Which was as true as he could make it.

"Must have been a trip and a half."

"It was. That piece of wire she's got for a gate. I forgot it was there."

Laura squeezing his arm, giving him the panics in another direction, Bill's hand still bearing down. "Between the two of us, mate, does she know you're out?"

"Of course she does."

"Are you sure? She'll skin you alive if you've ducked off without letting her know."

"Of course she knows."

"Say, Harry. Do you hear this? She let him out. She's never let any of them out before."

Josh unhappily hemmed in, the wave losing its momentum as if by agreement, kids gathering round, Harry reaching out a hand for Laura's arm and breaking her hold with determined strength that Josh could feel. Josh not sure about Harry, not sure; Harry saying, "What did you do, Joshua? Run off when she wasn't looking? She's not going to be pleased." All those grinning kids, all those faces he didn't have names for. Too many faces, too many grins, and all different now. He'd known they'd be different when Aunt Clara wasn't around. Trying to edge his shoulder out from under Bill's hand, but Bill wasn't letting go. "Is that why you tripped, mate? Were you running off in too much of a hurry to see? She'll flay you alive. You've broken the Sabbath, mate; that's what you've done. On Sundays *you* stay at home!"

Bill wasn't laughing, not exactly, but the look on his face Josh didn't like at all. Even Betsy was becoming part of the scene, twirling a towel, her hip bent gipsy-style. She'd not fronted up to him before, had treated him as if he wasn't there. "A Plowman? Who's kidding who?" Betsy sounding grown-up and nasal and not very nice. "Was there ever a Plowman kid with the guts to break out of bounds? And we've seen them all, haven't we just? She's let him out. The heat must be getting her down."

Josh feeling wounded, something inside him hurting many ways, hurting for Betsy for being less than she ought to be, hurting for Aunt Clara, hurting for himself and even for his crummy cousins who were too far away to speak up for themselves. These kids, Josh, they're not your kind. These kids. These lousy two-faced kids. Dragging his shoulder from under Bill's hand and elbowing out through the middle of them, pointing his elbows, thrusting with them, striking ribs and flesh and bone.

Josh walking uphill alone.

"Hey, Joshua, hey! What are you doing?" Harry's voice with command in it and surprise. "Can't you take a joke? Hey, don't go off in a huff."

Josh not bothering to look around. "The name is not Joshua, it's Josh! And my idea of a joke is something that makes you laugh." Not shouting, but knowing he was heard, and not breaking stride. They could do as they pleased. Jump on him from behind. Tear him down. He didn't care.

But no one came.

10

Standing on her garden path, sun beating on his head, feeling his hair blowing back in the wind. Standing there trembling, waiting for her to look up.

Aunt Clara in her cane chair framed by rose-laden veranda posts, with a closed book in her lap, open-fingered hand lying over it to keep it shut perhaps. Aunt Clara with her head bowed, wind in her hair too, stiff white hair, agitated like grass. Looking aged and small and insignificant, not at all like the woman who had commanded the respect, face to face, of a church hall full of kids who were different behind her back.

Gosh, Aunt Clara, look up. I've come this far and that's no small effort. Aren't you going to help? It's been awful hard getting back. It would have been dead easy to side with those kids, I could have gone their way, no trouble; but I've cut them off. That Betsy; I've cut her off too. First girl I've ever looked at much. I could have watched her swim, could have talked to her perhaps, could have found out whether that horrible voice is a big act or not. Like you said, Aunt Clara, no one's perfect. ...

Aunt Clara raising her head, meeting his eyes across the gap. No surprise on her face, no anger, no arrogance. Just looking at him with a face conveying nothing. Nothing there to draw him in or send him farther back.

Gosh, Aunt Clara, I don't know what it is, this thing about the

Plowmans, something to do with family I guess. I'd not reckoned on it, honest. We do mean something to each other, I'm blowed if I know what, it's got me bluffed.

Aunt Clara putting her book aside. His book; he could see that now. Leaving it on the barrel for him to pick up. Then getting to her feet. Funny the way she went about it; funny self-conscious way of standing up.

Don't go inside, Aunt Clara. If you go inside you'll make it harder still. You'll have me crawling to you then and you couldn't want me to do that.

I'm all lost. What does a fellow do next? I've never had a thundering row with Mum. Only with those rotten cousins, they're the only ones. *You've* had them here, you must know what they're like. What went wrong, Aunt Clara? It happened at the start. Were you really picking at me? I don't know. Maybe you were cracking jokes. I was too dog-tired to tell the difference. I'm not blaming anyone, you or me or anyone else. It was just the way it went. Aren't you going to say something? Aren't you going to help? I don't know whether you want me or not. But you must have got round to realizing you know more about Josh Plowman than anyone else? Those poems, Aunt Clara. You really shouldn't have taken them. You really should have waited. They're all the things a boy doesn't talk about. But knowing them the way you do; you and no one else.

Aunt Clara saying his name, "Josh." Not loading it up with sobs or turning it into an indictment, just saying it so quietly it was a wonder it wasn't lost.

Josh rushing up the path, Aunt Clara coming down, and somewhere in the middle they met.

"I'm sorry, Aunt Clara."

"You've forgiven me, Josh. God bless you for that. You're perfectly right; it was an awful thing I did. Do you understand,

Josh? I had to let you know I'd seen them. I couldn't put them back."

"Don't cry, Aunt Clara."

"I'm not crying, lad. But why have you taken so long to come? A real Plowman like your old Great-grandfather, one with heart. It's a long time I've been waiting for you to come up this path."

Gosh, Josh, fancy being sentimental and not minding it a bit.

MONDAY

11

Aunt Clara in the kitchen holding up the haversack, straps looped and ready for Josh to put on, smiling at his wonderment, talking in an undertone. "Why look so surprised? I said they'd come and right on time. We couldn't *expect* them yesterday afternoon, I told you that. Mr. Stockdale frightens them away; the dear old man rambles so. Now when they ask about the cricket match you agree. Have you got everything? Tighten the haversack—tighter than that; thirty years old and your father used it often. What do you think of that? *He's coming, boys. Just fastening his pack.* Be yourself, Josh. No tensions now. Join in and have fun." Aunt Clara kissing him on the cheek, that wet kiss. "Off you go! I'll not come to the door. This old gown has had its day; it's not decent enough."

Aunt Clara, you don't know the half of it, you don't know the half of it. But there was nothing he could say. All night I've been dreading this. All night I've been dreading it if they came. These kids. It's not because of Mr. Stockdale that I'm surprised. But there was nothing Josh could put into words, nothing he could do except give her a smile and cross the lobby to the screen door. Three faceless figures out there silhouetted against the light. Thank heaven only three. Josh had feared a crowd. Bill and Harry and someone he didn't know, Harry opening the door and with a foot nudging at the mass of fur. "Move yourself, old George. Come on, old fat cat.

Hey, don't you scratch. What do you feed him on, Miss Plowman? Lead shot? Hi there, Joshua."

"She's not coming to the door."

Harry looked faintly surprised.

"She's not dressed yet, that's all."

Bill giving him the same sort of look, maybe of doubt, maybe of surprise, but sounding off loudly, full of beans. "Step big there, mate, or you'll iron the old man into the mat. Bye, Miss Plowman! We're going out to Mitchell's place. Should be back about four. Come on, you lot, we'll cut down the back way and save a few yards."

Josh trying to believe in them and to front up to each of them open-faced, but knowing it was a lie, trying to place the third of them, a floppy-haired twelve-year-old looking hollow-eyed but so like Betsy it could hardly be true. Bill guessing Josh's mind. "This is the kid brother, the terror of Ryan Creek. You didn't see him yesterday. He had a belly-ache. Sicker than sick, weren't you, Rex, but he's not telling why."

"Not on your sweet life." Rex with a giggle in his voice, as if perhaps a giggle was almost there. A wild-looking kid but so like Betsy, so like her that Josh didn't know where to put his eyes, hardly noticing that Harry was making an effort to sound as if everyone had been mates for years. "It's a beaut day, Joshua, better than yesterday."

Crowding down the path almost in a heap, as if they were escaping from the scene of a crime and were anxious to be somewhere else to commit the next. Josh feeling they were pressing him too close again, too close all the time, pushing him with numbers. When people came separately he could hold his own; even Bill on his own, gun and all, would be different from Bill in a crowd. Harry still harping on the weather, "Yesterday was a real dog, wasn't it? I hate wind. Gets everyone down. Like a madhouse at home. Everyone in a bad mood." Josh getting the twitch; Harry working on him all right; Harry softening him up for the big crawl down. If Aunt Clara thought they lived on the surface out in the sun, she could bally well think it.

"Watch the wire here, mate. Don't dive turkey over top again." Bill sounding extra friendly and young Rex holding up the wire with a cheeky grin, like Betsy's grin on the train, Josh ducking underneath and suddenly sprawling, one ankle rapping into the other, his haversack rearing up and cracking him in the back of the neck and pitching him flat on his face.

"Holy mackerel!" Bill's incredulous voice. "How'd he get down there?"

Josh almost leaping to his feet, coughing and rubbing at his neck and cursing himself, young Rex grinning so widely it was a wonder his face didn't split, Harry looking bewildered as if it had happened to himself and glancing uneasily up to the house, Bill trying not to laugh. "You've got talent, mate. How about one more time, slowed down?"

Rex giggling his head off, but Josh had a long way to go before he'd be laughing when Bill O'Connor cracked a joke.

"Did you trip him, Rex?" Harry putting more into it than a simple question.

"Of course he didn't." Bill sounding rough. "This bloke's talent is all his own. You haven't got anything wrong with you, Joshua, like loose nuts and bolts or a tin hip?"

Rex's stupid giggling wasn't giving Josh a chance and he'd have paid a pocketful to have landed him one in the middle of his nose, but hitting that face would be like hitting Betsy. Josh snarling, "You saw what happened. I tripped."

"You don't have to tell us that, mate."

"Well so what, so what! What's so funny about it? Are we going to hang round here, or are we going to get going?"

"Sure, mate, sure, but it's five miles out to Mitchell's place and five miles back. Do you reckon you can make it? We'll look good bringing you home on a stretcher. This is only the back gate!"

Harry wailing, "Bill, give it away, will you! What's wrong with you kids? I'll clout you, Rex, if you don't shut up. If he tripped he tripped. Isn't that good enough? Let's get out of here. She'll see us from the house."

Josh almost sneering. "And that'd be real bad, wouldn't it?"

"Yeh! It would!"

"Tripped?" Bill was trying to make a laugh out of it, still trying, but he must have known he had pushed it too far. "Twice, so help me. Two days running. In the same place."

Josh shrilling, "For Pete's sake, why make a thing of it? Haven't you ever tripped? Do *you* always get up laughing when you knock the wind out of yourself? Look, after yesterday, I don't care whether I come with you kids or not. You're not doing me a favour."

"You can say that again, mate, the favour's not for you, make no mistake. Betsy's right. There never was a Plowman kid worth a second try."

"Meaning what?"

"Meaning whatever you think."

Harry still attempting to make the peace. "Give it away. Knock it off; will you!" Harry getting very agitated. "Strike me, Bill, we're at her back gate."

But Bill was turning savage. "What difference does that make? She knows by now. He's told her, I bet, with everything twisted back-to-front. She wouldn't even come to the door. Not dressed yet? Bunk. Have you ever known her not to come to the door? I told you that big act he put on didn't mean a thing. He doesn't care about her or about us. These Plowman kids are all tarred with the same brush. I'm sick of molly-coddling them. Why should I have to? And this one's so wet he can't even stand up."

Harry turning on Rex. "You and your stupid giggle. You and your quick feet. Now look what you've started. Strike me, I thought we had a chance of patching it up."

Something inside Josh was running wild and he could feel himself dragging off his haversack and wrestling with the straps, blood rushing to his head and violence rushing to his hands, and Harry rushing in the middle. "Don't you touch him, Bill, you lay off. He'll kill you, Joshua, he's twice your size. Not here, Bill, not here, Bill, *have some sense.*" Harry pushing Bill in the chest, almost pushing him flat, dragging at young Rex by the wrist and shepherding them both off; Josh still trying to get his haversack off; frustrated by the straps, infuriated by the straps, caught up in them like a strait jacket, Harry, Bill and Rex going beyond reach, going towards the station road, Harry looking back with an open-mouth grimace as if he couldn't get his breath, Rex laughing, laughing out of sight.

"Oh, that's great! That's absolutely great! Every day the thirteenth of the month!"

Josh flung his haversack into the dirt, and he would have kicked it like a football except that Dad had worn it thirty years ago and it was full of lunch.

12

So what did you do with a day that ended a few minutes after nine instead of at four o'clock? Four o'clock, Bill had yelled they'd be back. He couldn't go up to the house and fix her in the eye and say, "I've changed my mind," or "They've changed their minds," or "I feel sick," or "We had a fight." One thing would lead to another and when he told lies he could never act the part.

"Josh," Mum always said, "with a face like yours you've got to tell the truth."

Yesterday he could walk back into the house and ignore what had happened down the track. He could march off with her to church, clothes spick and span again, perfectly sponged and pressed, *knowing* the kids wouldn't come but not having to say a word because she had no knowledge of what had taken place. He could sit in that huge dining-room at a table set for ten eating egg-and-bacon pie and spicy fruit cake and still not have to confess, because she made all the excuses and looked for none from him. Yesterday had its problems. Today was a different kettle of fish.

"Be yourself, no tensions now. Join in and have fun." Or something like that. Something like that she'd said. How about that? Join in and have fun. Ha, ha. What are you laughing at, Josh? I'm having fun.

So he kicked the pack despite Dad, who'd worn it, and his lunch. Slinging it to his shoulder again by one strap, wondering whether the lemon squash would dribble out, shaking it to hear whether the bottle was whole or in bits.

Have fun. Have fun doing what? I pay that for this year's joke. I haven't put a mean word on anyone, not a word out of place. I've played fair by you, Aunt Clara, and fair by them. But it's getting tougher by the minute. I've even played fair by my rotten cousins and what a lot of crumbs they've turned out to be, as if I hadn't guessed. They've been stirring up some strife round this neck of the woods. For Pete's sake! She hasn't had one in the house for eighteen months!

Such nice boys, waiting anxiously for me to come! They've been waiting all right; they had me dead and buried before I hit the place. Gosh, Aunt Clara, you must know what they're like. How could you live here all your life and not wake up to facts? But they're so nice to her face. I can't work them out. Marching with her up the street. Marching down again. Crowding round her. Carrying her books. Yes, Miss Plowman. No, Miss Plowman. How's your stove wood holding out? Do you need any chopped? Tuesday morning, Miss Plowman, for the scrubbing this week? Those kids have got me tossed.

Walking through the long grass trapping burrs in his boot-laces and seeds like darts in his socks. Swinging wide of those bleary-eyed cows with their horns like hooks.

You've got to get away somewhere, Josh. Can't hang round here or some grown-up will spot you and go trotting off to Aunt Clara. "What's your nephew doing down the back on his lonesome ownsome looking as miserable as a wet week?"

Suddenly thinking of snakes.

Jumping Jehosaphat!

What a ghastly thought, without kids like Bill and Harry and Rex to bear the brunt of the attack. Snakes wouldn't bite them anyway; the bite would kill the snake.

13

The importance of decision, Josh, becomes a pressing matter. Like what do you do with yourself?

Stand there and be gored by cows, stand here and be seen by inquisitive grown-ups, or go bush and be savaged by snakes. Keep your sense of humour, Josh. You could die of old age and think of the years that might take.

Josh sneaking down to the railway station trying to look like someone else. Hiding by the creek under the footbridge of planks where he had stubbed a toe on Saturday night.

Ryan Creek Visit. Syllabus for Monday: bridge party for one. Bring your own lunch and keep out of sight. Return to quarters at four o'clock and lie your head off about it. Syllabus for the rest of the week? As for Monday, repeat.

Recalling Dad's words: "Good snake country, Ryan Creek. The original Snake Pit. They breed 'em long and thick and tough. They tan their hides and use 'em for armour-plating battleships." There were times when Dad still had to grow up. "Remember, Josh, carry a stick in the bush and keep your eyes peeled along the creek."

Listening to the babbling of the brook with reeds on the banks and grass three feet high at least and rustlings and hissings and buzzings, not knowing which was which, animal, insect, reptile, or fish.

Tragic Death of Poet

Josh, fourth-generation Plowman of the well-known Pioneering Plowmans who in 1853 started hacking Ryan Creek out of the Primeval Bush, was found today under a footbridge, Twin Punctures in the flesh of his rump where he sat. One fourth-generation Pioneering Plowman now extinct. Will be remembered for an Unpublished Volume of Verse and a sonnet, "Christmas Morning at Gumtree Flat," printed in the Children's Columns of this newspaper on 24th December. Also for his Undefeated 21 Runs Not Out scored against Green House Thirds last November twelve months.

"Hullo, Joshua."

Jumping almost a foot.

That red-haired little monster of eight who carried Aunt Clara's books popping up out of the reeds like a Jack-in-a-box, with a string in his hand tied to a lump of meat. "I'm catching yabbies, I am."

Josh swallowing back his fright and endeavouring to give the impression he sat under footbridges every day of the week muttering to himself.

"Yabbies don't live here. They live in the dam, they do."

Josh, in a scattered way, trying to think about that. "Shouldn't you be fishing there then?"

"Yabbies nip."

"Perhaps I understand, perhaps I don't."

"What are you doing, Joshua?"

He had been scared of that. "Do you mind calling me Josh?"

"What are you doing, Josh?"

"Writing a poem."

"Without a pencil or a book?"

"You're fishing for yabbies, aren't you, where there aren't any yabbies to catch?"

"You're hiding."

"I'm not."

"I heard you talking to yourself."

"That's the poem. Getting it right. You do it in your head first."

"I saw you coming down the hill. I saw you looking back. You had a fight, didn't you, with Harry and Bill and Rex?"

"I did not."

"They went *that* way. They were talking a lot. They were cross."

"There wasn't any fight and don't you go saying there was. You couldn't see a thing from here. You'd need eyes on stalks twenty feet up."

"Have you got a penny?"

"Why?"

"If I had a penny I'd buy a liquorice strap, I would. Then I'd eat it and not tell anyone."

"There's nothing to tell!"

"I'd like a penny, I would. Your auntie doesn't like boys who fight."

The little crumb. You wouldn't have thought butter would melt in his mouth. Digging down for the penny and, breathing hard and chucking it at him.

"You'd better not go *that* way. That's where *they* went."

"Look, Sonny, I gave you the penny because you're a nice boy. I don't care which way they went."

Josh deliberately walking *that* way, asserting his manhood.

Coming back onto the road where a bluestone ford crossed the creek, water running inches deep. Only birds in flight could have got to the other side with dry feet, but there were fates worse than water-sogged boots.

"You'd better not go along the creek."

Why couldn't the monster keep his mouth shut? Wild-looking country down there, real scrubby stuff cut through by a narrow track swarming with snakes and spiders and bull-ants and three kids he didn't want to meet. A quick glance back and the red head was still blooming in the grass.

"That's right, Josh. That's where they went. Down the creek."

Talk about sticking your neck in a noose. Yelling back at him, "I told you I don't care. Get that into your thick skull."

Deliberately striding it out along the track instead of crossing the ford, haversack bouncing on his shoulders, heart going thump, hoping if he looked as if he was heading for somewhere important the snakes would let him pass, ears cocked for hisses, but hearing Sonny's parting shout: "Don't put your foot in a trap."

"In a *what*?" But not out loud; shrieks of horror like that you kept to yourself. What sort of trap? For rabbits, for foxes, for city kids who spent half the day tumbling "turkey over top"? Surely they didn't stick traps in the middle of tracks? Iron claws that went snap? Pits six feet deep, with brush over the top and spikes underneath?

Well, if not like that, like what? A trap's a trap.

Another quick glance back. Red head gone. Everything gone except bush. What a life. Hanging on to a tree for a bit of moral support and breaking down a likely branch, not too thin, not too thick, to prepare a weapon for the fight to the death, shocking hard work, nearly busting himself, then stripping off the leaves and the twigs and giving the mangled-looking stick a couple of trial whacks against the trunk to make sure it wouldn't break. If Mum could see her darling boy she'd drop dead. Trying very hard to view his condition in a philosophical light and giving a wry smile to impress any ancestors who might have been haunting the creek, there being no fewer than seven assorted Plowmans buried thereabouts. Trying not to behave like a lily-livered twit, but labouring under difficulties, because if you are a lily-livered twit that's that, no use pretending you're not.

Imagine these characters, Josh, who catch snakes by the tail and crack them dead like a whip. They must be nuts. Imagine these characters who hunt crocodiles for the fun of it when they could be at home curled up with a book! Imagine Great-grandfather Plowman in 1853 leading his packhorse by the snout, hacking his way through the bush, coming to this very spot with a joyful shout, Crown Allotment something or other, acres of it everywhere lying miles out of sight, paid for in hard-won gold from the gambling tents of Ballarat. Great-grandfather Plowman standing hands on hips in the wild primeval bush taking time off from history to paint a picture of himself. Or did he paint it later on? But what went wrong? How come all he left his family was a house on the hill, six weatherboard cottages in the High Street, fourteen self-portraits, and fifty thousand mining shares worth less than the paper they were written on? What happened to the rest? Great-grandfather Plowman must also have been a twit.

Josh looking heavenwards, checking for thunderbolts, then striding off again, eyes darting all ways at once, ears alert, nostrils a-twitch, hoping not to antagonize the snakes with his wattle stick, swinging it carelessly as if he intended it only for swaggering with or for leaning on or for knocking country kids on the head, which, as far as those kids were concerned, was a definite risk.

Don't put your foot in a trap!

Honest to goodness, what next?

Looking for pits and snares and nets in the tree-tops, then stopping suddenly to the sound of a wild scuffle in the bush, a clinking sound like a chain being dragged across itself, a cry like an agonized baby that made him feel sick, a terrible cry, awful, awful, like nothing he had ever heard in his life, so close that the hairs bristled on his neck, so close that he would have fled if his body had not drained from the shock.

Standing motionless, his heartbeat leaping up to meet shouts that came from somewhere else.

"Hear that?"

"Did I what!"

"Yippeee! What have we got?"

Josh heard them running, heard them coming, Harry, Bill and Rex.

14

Harry crashing up the track ahead of the others, seeing Josh, and recoiling as if an invisible mass had struck him head-on and twisted him out of shape. Harry shrieking, "It's not you! You're not caught!" Bill and Rex overtaking him, floundering one into the other. "*He's not caught?*"

Harry groaning and looking at Josh's feet and sagging from the shoulders and putting fingertips to his eyes as if a sharp pain was registering there.

"I'm sorry to disappoint you." Josh not meaning it really, scarcely knowing he said it.

Bill shouting, "Don't be a fool. What a stupid thing to say. What a right stupid thing to say. What *is* caught then? Where is it? You set this one, Rex. Where'd you put it?"

Harry groaning.

Bill still shouting, "Where's the trap, Rex? Snap out of it. Snap out of it. Find it."

"I don't know where it is, Bill. I can't remember. You told me to shift it."

"Five minutes ago. In five minutes you can't remember a thing like that?" Bill dragging the scrub aside in all directions, jumping from place to place.

Rex whining, "What's the panic? What's the panic?"

"I said find it!"

Harry coming out of his fright and wading into the bush off the track, Josh following him, hoping he was going the wrong way, hoping to escape from the physical presence of the ghastly cry that had come and gone, had quite gone, but went on shattering him, turning the earth where he stood into an unhealthy place. *Primitive* was the word Mum would have used. Harry suddenly throwing out his arms as if holding back a crowd. "It's here. It's a beauty. A big fat beauty."

Josh not wanting to look, dreading it, but drawn in despite himself, even pushed on towards it by the pressure of Bill and Rex. A narrow track in the scrub as if made by tiny men, an arch knee-high in wire-grass as if woven for shelter and security, in it a rabbit, brown and white, caught by one foreleg between rusty iron jaws, dragging the trap on a frantic arc, eyes huge with terror but making no cry, clanking on the chain, scuffling in the dust, Rex exclaiming, "Strike me. Silly as a rabbit. Five minutes! He must have watched me set it. How dumb can you get? Didn't even wait till dark."

Josh unable to move, not wanting to think, dying to get down on his knees, dying to let it go free, even free on three legs, caring like mad for the desperate little creature, but unable to move.

Harry holding out a hand. "Here, give me your stick. Joshua, your stick!"

Harry taking it and with it peeling the grass back, Rex jumping up and down, "Here, you lay off, Harry. Give it to me. It's my rabbit. I set the trap."

"Go away. Let the expert do it."

Bill edging round. "He's a savage little brute."

Harry laying the grass aside until the arch was quite gone.

"Let me do it, Harry. It's my rabbit. Go on, go on. Don't be mean."

"It's got to be done properly."

"I can do it properly. I can do it."

"Yeh, I've seen you at it. Give a man the horrors. Shut him up, Bill."

The stick flashing down striking the rabbit in the neck, tearing Josh apart. Tears he couldn't stop starting from his eyes and the rabbit jerking a dozen or more times and lying still, lying lifeless, blood on its mouth.

I'm sorry, little rabbit. I'm sorry. But what could I do?

Harry handing back the stick and Rex swooping, getting his heel on the pressure plate and releasing the iron jaws. "What a beauty." Holding it up by the hind legs as limp as a rag. Bill suddenly blocking the view, Bill full-face meeting Josh in the eye. "You all right, mate? Look at Joshua, Harry. White as a sheet."

Josh trying to speak but choked for words.

"It's only a rabbit, mate. Only a rabbit."

Josh hurling his stick away. "It didn't have a chance. You could have let it go."

"Let it go?" Bill laughing, as honestly as anyone could. "You must be joking. Let it go? What are you? Some sort of a crank? Cleaner meat this way, mate. No shot to spit out on the plate."

"I'll never eat rabbit again. I'll never eat a rabbit again. Not as long as I live."

"Oh, come off it, Joshua. Don't make a martyr of it. I killed it clean and quick."

"Yeh, if you'd not heard it cry—"

"Cry? Are you wasting sympathy on a rabbit?"

"If you'd not heard it cry you'd have come back tonight maybe; maybe you'd have come back tomorrow; or maybe not at all. Would it have still been clean and quick?" Josh walking away, walking faster and faster. Running. Breaking through the bush. Then throwing himself down and weeping, but not ashamed because he wept; ashamed only because it had been his stick handed over as if he didn't care. Doing nothing. Standing by. Letting it happen.

15

Yesterday after lunch for half an hour before church Aunt Clara had sat at her organ and played hymns from memory with her glasses off. Sat at her organ and pedalled and played and smiled. She looked happy; no one miserable could have looked as happy as that. Tall, thin organ (six feet tall? eight feet tall? should have toppled on its face) with miniature columns all over it holding up shelves and miniature balustrades to stop things falling off; mirrors all over it catching reflections, eye-to-eye reflections—some of them as she sought out his face. Could she see him without her glasses, or was he only a shadow or a shape? She was happy; in a way so was Josh. "It was God's will," she had said, startling him at the time. "Praise Him for bringing you back."

Sometimes she would finish a hymn and talk a while, knowing he was listening in.

"Hymns are nice. I'm getting too old to play anything else. My fingers are stiff. Hymns are simple sounds to send out on the wind. Here I am, Lord, hear me, adding a little to your world this day instead of always taking for myself."

Playing again. Talking again.

"We're only children after all. He knows it's a mysterious world. He knows He has filled it with questions that may tease and trouble us. I wonder whether we demand clearer answers of ourselves than He intends or expects?"

Playing again, for five minutes perhaps.

"Don't torment yourself, Josh. You'll burn yourself out. Have a little faith in His universe, in the order He has given it, in His beauty and justice. He hopes for us to accept His love and fit in. The great poets are men of simple faith. It pains Him to watch us beating our heads against the rocks."

No, no, no, no, Aunt Clara.

All wrong yesterday. All wrong today.

We'd still be in the trees swinging from limb to limb. We'd still have hair all over us and fleas to scratch. But you believe God snapped his fingers and there we were, all fashioned and finished. No, Aunt Clara. Not like that. Much harder than that; much prouder than that. Mum says we made God much more than he ever made us. Why praise him for sending me back to you? I went back myself. Praising *him* for that makes me out to be less. It's by weeping and wailing, it's by fighting back, it's by breaking your heart, it's by hating yourself because you didn't help a rabbit; that's what God is, Aunt Clara. Mum says God is in yourself and I reckon she's right. I've thought about these things, I've thought and thought.

I can't help it if I burn myself up. I'd rather cry for a little rabbit than kill thousands of ancient Egyptians who worshipped someone else. What do these kids care about a rabbit when you tell them God does that? Some kids are like me and some are like them, I guess. I don't suppose they can help it either, taking things as they come, living out in the sun. But if there's got to be a sun, Aunt Clara, there's got to be a shadow. I reckon I'd rather have my kind of shadow.

I reckon you're terrific, Aunt Clara, honest I do, because those poems must have given you a shock. I mean, you're an old maid, never married or anything like that. Those poems; they'll not be printing *them* on the kid's page in the *Herald* on a Saturday night.

Yet you understood better than Dad; that's got me tossed. And I know why you took them to read, I've got to be fair, you thought I'd brought them for that, and I'd flaked out on that bed, sound asleep. Gosh, Aunt Clara, you must have had a shock. But what about that rabbit? What about everything else? What about me when I was a little kid out in the sun pouring boiling water on ants crawling over the front step? What a horrible thing to do. Even Mum couldn't have cared. Where would I have got the kettle from? She must have known what I was at.

Can I cry for little ants, too? Can I cry now because I didn't cry then?

You can play hymns on your organ and for you that makes it right.

16

Sitting on the ground hugging his knees, sniffing because he couldn't sharpen himself up enough to pull out a handkerchief. Where had he got himself? Huddled in the scrub with sunlight flickering on his neck, all wrapped about with bush. "Good snake country, Ryan Creek. The original Snake Pit." Those reptiles must have been taking the morning off to clean their teeth.

Coming back to the day and the instant. Getting on top. Feeling a bit better.

I wept for you, rabbit. Someone cared.

Blowing his nose. *Baaarp.*

Aunt Clara's right, you know. I'll burn myself out.

Blowing it again like a motor-bus. *Baaarp.*

What'll those kids think? I don't care what they think. How could I have gone shooting? Me with a shotgun, with any kind of gun? If they'd handed it to me I'd have turned it on them. One for the road up the seat of their pants.

Staggering round a bit, trying to find a way out of the bush.

I'm going to be a vegetarian. I'll eat nuts. I'll chew lettuce leaves. I've had an *experience*, that's what. Talk about funny peculiar. Am I going to be a mystic or something? The Right Reverend Josh Plowman, the mad monk. Lives in a rabbit warren at Gumtree Flat. Eats nuts. Trance starts daily at ten o'clock. Everyone welcome to inspect. Admission free. Penny in the poor-box on the way out.

For Pete's sake. The awful things that could happen to a fellow when he grows up.

Drifting along the track beside the babbling brook.

If you're a monk you're not allowed to have a wife. Me and Betsy. How about that? Married to the *voice*. Send her to elocution classes. How now brown cow and all that stuff. Betsy and me. That'd be the life.

Walking light of foot listening hard for kids. No more rabbits in traps, please. No more traps. How many of the filthy things did they set? Cicadas starting up, cicadas or crickets, throbbing like a heartbeat. A wall of earth at a distance on the other side of the creek. The railway embankment. The one for swaying on as the train gallops into town winning back a minute of the many it has lost.

Poor little rabbit. I hope you're full of bones that stick in their throats.

You see, Aunt Clara, I'm going to be a poet. A fellow came to school once. He wasn't like the fellows who usually come to speak. Not a footballer or a cricketer or a policeman or a parson with his collar round back-to-front. A fellow all bent, leaning on a stick. You've got to get hurt, he said, if you want to write books. When you cry you cry for someone else. When you laugh you laugh at yourself. When you're cruel it's your own life you tear to bits. There he was, Aunt Clara, all stooped and bent, poking fun at himself. He had us in fits. When I grow up I'd like to be like that. He was looking straight at me half the time. I think he must have guessed. Most of the other kids were taken aback. In the middle of all those laughs, you know, coming out with a thing like that.

Josh stopping, realizing that Great-grandfather was staring him in the face, Josh caught by surprise, not sure what to think. Great-grandfather's bridge standing there ahead, standing there since 1882, standing there still, waiting for Josh. "Well, what do you know!" The family pride and the family joke.

Not a bad-looking effort at that, Great-grandfather, though I'll bet you never raised a sweat. All you'd have been raising was your screaming voice telling them where to put what next. How come you never painted it for the mantelshelf with yourself in the picture holding it up?

And so, dear friends, the railway comes to Ryan Creek, thanks to the father of the town who got himself elected to Parliament for that and nothing else. Great-grandfather riding on the footplate, top-hat and tails and coal dust all over his face. "Now," Great-grandfather booms to the cheering multitude gathered about, "on rails of steel and hearts of oak Ryan Creek goes forth. Today we're on the map; tomorrow we become a metropolis." What went wrong, Great-grandfather? Did someone miscalculate?

Josh running down the track to the yellow road at the foot, pack thudding on his shoulder-blades shortening his breath, excited, surprised at himself. That long bridge with its graceful curve breaking the embankment through west to east, that long bridge with its huge logs set in earth and rock, logs knitted in the air like lace, that long bridge spanning creek and dam and yellow road and bush.

"It's beautiful, Great-grandfather."

Imagine that old man working it out to the last nut and bolt. Never built a bridge before in his life. Sitting down in that house up there on the hill—at the very desk, Josh, where you sat last night—making it up out of his own grey head. Imagine the engineer in Melbourne town, a long way off; long years back, poring over it for hours, working out this and considering that, scratching his neck, Great-grandfather waiting silent and tense. Imagine the engineer at last looking up: "Yes, Mr. Plowman, sir. A minor problem in the curve, we'll sort it out. Sink the piles six feet more if we don't strike rock, and I can see it outliving us. If this is the bridge you want, this is the bridge you'll get. Remarkable, Mr. Plowman, sir.

Josh standing there agape, family legend coming to life.

"You were quite a fellow, Great-grandfather. Maybe the Plowmans are right. Mum ought to come and see this. She shouldn't poke fun at you so much."

Harry, Bill and Rex. There they were a distance off; their backs to the sun, their backs to Josh. Thank heaven for that. Heading down the yellow road, a yellow distance, sun-baked stubble of harvested wheat, framed by the bridge Great-grandfather built. Broad water beneath that bridge lying disturbed and clouded as if at an earlier hour it might have mirrored the logs knitted overhead and the wattles round about and one patch of fresh growing grass at the edge. No pictures in the water now, only ripples and swirls of mud and a heavy girl in a green bathing-suit standing more than waist-deep.

"Hullo, Joshua."

Bet your life, Josh. Bet your life on it. Think aloud, speak to yourself, and the world is listening in.

Josh sighing. "Hullo, Laura." Poor, unattractive thing. Got nothing at all. You certainly missed out, Laura. It's a shame. Where were you when all the charms were handed out? "What are you doing there? Isn't it early for swimming?"

Laura giggling. "I said I'd catch you, Joshua, didn't I?"

"I don't remember that."

"I said it yesterday. I said it twice.

"Not to me you didn't. You must have said it to someone else."

"Don't be cross with me, Joshua."

"Well, call me *Josh*. You've no idea what that other word does to me!"

"Miss Plowman calls you Joshua."

"Not any more she doesn't, and if you'd gone to church you'd have realized it." Josh wanting to get away from her.

"You're masterful."

"I'm *what*?"

"Different from yesterday. I felt sorry for you then." What could you say to that? "Look, Laura, you couldn't have been standing there when I came along. I couldn't be as blind as that."

Laura taking a great gulp of air and sliding from sight, Josh grumbling to himself. "Yes, so I ask a silly question!"

Waiting.

"All right, all right. So you ducked under water. Now you can come up."

Waiting.

"Is she a seal or something?"

Getting restless. Beginning to count. Skipping the first twenty. Starting at twenty-one.

"For Pete's sake, Laura, come up, will you! You'll burst."

Clouds in the water turning yellow, distinctly yellow.

"Godfathers. She's stuck. She's snagged. *Laura*." Josh forgetting the count and tearing off his pack and in vain trying to tear off his boots. "Holy cow! What do you do when you can't swim?" Floundering down to the water's edge, slipping and slithering in the mud and suddenly there she was, green head like an acorn bobbing out in the middle, green cap in a yellow swirl.

"You crazy loon! You complete nut! You scared the life out of me."

"Coming in for a swim?"

"No, I'm not."

"The water's beaut."

"It doesn't look much to me. Dirty great pool of mud."

"I do it all the time when I'm on my own."

Josh wading up the bank again, trying not to slip, still shaking like a leaf, suddenly hearing what she said. "Do what?"

"Out in the middle where it's deep. Down on the bottom. I stir it up. The kids go crook."

"You stir up that mud! You do it on purpose? It's a wonder they
don't kill you. You'll give yourself a disease or something."

Laura was back in the shallows again.

"I dive from the bridge, too."

"You're cracked. You'll break your neck!"

"Come on. Come in."

"I said no."

"Can't you swim?"

"Of course I can swim. But I don't carry a bathing-costume in
my pocket. I'm not swimming in the raw."

"The boys would."

"I'm sure they would, but I won't."

"What are you putting your haversack on your back for?"

"Where else would I put it?"

She came splashing up to the bank with movements surpris-
ingly feminine, slipping off her bathing-cap, shaking free her hair,
standing, perhaps sinking into mud ankle-deep. "Don't go away,
Josh."

"I'm out for a hike. I'm not hiking if I stay here. I only came
to see the bridge."

"Maximilian Plowman's bridge."

Josh flinching. "Yeh. I believe they called him that."

"But you were going with the boys."

"I might have been."

Laura looking away, as if wishing to spare him from something.
"Harry told me."

"There wasn't any secret about it."

"About the rabbit? About crying because of a rabbit?"

Josh going tight, his breath catching. "And you wouldn't, I
suppose?"

"Because of a silly old rabbit? You're funny, Josh, aren't you?"

"Yeah, I'm a scream."

Heading for the road and hearing her call. "I'm sorry ... I didn't mean it, Josh. Don't go."

Not bothering to look back. "I can't see any reason for wanting to stay."

Stranded, if that was the word, on the road, assessing which escape to take, on through the bridge and into the perils of the yellow distance in one direction or back the other way probably slap into the middle of the High Street. What a choice. What a life. Yet beginning to feel bad, uncomfortably so, as if he might have committed a cruelty as callous as the death of the rabbit. Not the same kind of cruelty, but as deliberate as the flashing stick. "I shouldn't have said that. Not to her. Not like that."

Going back to the dam, looking for her, not calling for her but speaking her name. "Laura."

Where the heck had she gone? Not to the bottom again! At the edge of the scrub with a dirty-looking towel and an armful of clothes and a face like a spaniel unjustly chastised. A moment of confusion, of deciding, then sitting himself down close to the water where patches of grass survived, staging a performance as if he intended to camp there for days. It was difficult with Laura, not knowing about her, not being sure. She could have been simple but might have been wise. Aunt Clara last night had put it in an odd way: "Laura Jones is a strange little girl." Not so much of the *little*, Aunt Clara, please.

Laura thinking about it. Thinking about something, anyway, her head bending to one side. To conceal a smile? You don't know, Josh, do you?

Laura crossing the intervening ground diverting her eyes. Laura sitting down a step away draped with her towel. What was going on in that head still bent to the side?

"Bill said looking after you was worse than minding a two-year-old."

Holy cow.

"Thanks, that's made my day."

"He said you'd gone home to your auntie. He said she ought to change your nappy, powder your bottom, and put you to bed."

Getting prickles round the collar and shivers down the spine. Thinking of all the noble thoughts that had brought him back to her. What a shocking waste of nobility.

"Bill's mad."

Josh swallowing hard. "I guess that's something."

"Rex said—"

"*I don't want to know what Rex said!*"

"It was funny."

"I'll bet it was. They're a real funny family, I don't think."

"What about Betsy? Don't you like her either?"

Walked into it! Straight into it! Finally, she'd made her point. All round the bushes, up and down the mountains—bang!

"Well, don't you?"

Josh sighing. "I didn't say that."

"I've seen you looking at her, all gooey-eyed."

"I'm allowed to look."

"They all look at Betsy."

Meaning, of course, that they never looked at Laura. "If you try to get Betsy, you'll have to fight Harry." "I'm not trying to 'get' Betsy. Where'd you pick up a cranky idea like that?"

"She's Harry's girl."

"Is she?"

"That's what Harry says, and she thinks you're wet."

"By golly, Laura, you're a real morale-builder you are."

"So you are trying to get her?"

"No, I'm not."

"She's beautiful, isn't she?"

"She's all right, Laura."

"But I'm fat."

"Look, Laura. ..." What could you do with her? "Do you want me to stay or not? You keep this up and I'll be off. Once and for all, I don't take any notice of girls, I've never had a girl friend, and I don't want one—Betsy, you, or anyone else."

"Well, stop making eyes at her. Because if you don't, Harry's going to bop you. And Harry bops good. He can flatten Bill like a tack. But I think you're nice.

Which was news almost as bad as Betsy's opinion that he was wet.

"Bill said you wouldn't come by. He said you'd gone home to your auntie and she ought—"

Interrupting. "I *know* what he said!"

"I've been waiting since half past eight."

His heart sinking because he knew the question had to be asked. "What for, Laura? Waiting for what?"

"For you to come by. And you did. I'm glad I stayed. They wanted me to go home. Harry was cross. He said I was chasing you and it was silly, but it's not silly because you're nice. Harry said a boy like you wouldn't look at me twice."

"Harry was cruel to say that."

"Harry cruel? Nah. Who cares? Because you walked away and came back. You're nice. I don't care if you are a sonk. I don't care if you did burst into tears because of a silly old rabbit. Kids who write poetry are like that, aren't they, Josh?"

"Gee, Laura, you've got a happy way of putting things." Feeling like they ought to push him out with the bargains and sell him off at half-price. Snapped up by Laura Jones. Rushed home and framed under glass. Hung over the fireplace.

"You haven't told me yet."

"You're ahead of me, Laura. Way ahead. Haven't told you what?"

"About your poems."

"Oh. ..." That was the bottom of the world, rock-bottom, falling out.

"You promised."

"Yeh, I know I did."

"But now you don't want to."

Turning to her, surprised. "What made you say that?"

"You don't want to, do you? You just don't."

"That's right. I don't."

"I wrote a poem when I was eleven. I haven't written another one. Mr. Cotton said I copied it and wouldn't give me any marks. The kids laughed."

"And you didn't copy it?"

"Spring is a happy season

Cold old winter has gone

The birds begin to build their nests

Up in the trees so high

Spring is happiest and the best

Of all the seasons that go by."

Josh sitting there, watching her cry.

"I didn't copy it."

Josh reaching out to her hand, and taking it, and holding it.

"I think it's lovely, Laura. Of course you didn't copy it."

17

Josh, what have you done?

Impulse will be the death of you yet.

Never held a girl by the hand in your life—not one that wasn't young enough to be your baby sister or old enough to be your mother. And you pick one that'll eat you up.

Josh, disengage.

Get your fingers out, Josh.

Holy cow, you've done it now. I mean, she's a sweet kid, a damsel in distress, behaved very nobly you did, a gentleman's first response, but she's got you now. Got her hooks in, Josh. Get your hand back.

"Laura, I've got an itch. I want to scratch."

"You've got your other hand, Josh."

"I'm right-handed, Laura. I can't scratch with my left."

"You're shy, aren't you? Do you really want your hand back?"

"It would help, Laura. It's a very bad itch."

"If you don't think about it, Josh, it'll go away."

"I'm very much afraid there's no hope."

"Josh, do you truly, truly think my poem's nice?"

"I do."

"Are yours like that?"

"No, Laura."

"He should have given me some marks.'

"Eight out of ten at least."

"You mean that?"

"Yes, Laura."

"I never had eight out of ten for anything."

"Eight out of ten, at least. You were eleven. And you'd never had eight out of ten for anything. Your teacher made a mistake."

"I say my poem lots and lots of times, over and over again to myself."

"Yes, Laura, but can I please have my hand back. It's just not right. I'm not old enough."

"Don't be silly. Of course you are. We have sweethearts here when we're ten."

"I'm sure Great-grandfather Plowman would be very upset to hear that. Where I live we wait till we grow up. Please, Laura, will you give me my hand back. If anyone comes and sees me like this I think I'll flip."

"They won't care. No one round here cares. They do it all the time."

"I think you're telling a fib. I haven't seen Harry and Betsy holding hands."

"Betsy won't."

"Why not?"

Laura, to his surprise, allowed his hand to fall.

"Why don't Betsy and Harry hold hands? Why don't they, Laura?"

But she wasn't answering and appeared to have shut her eyes, which was an annoying anticlimax, because Josh was so busily scratching himself he had developed a real-life itch.

"Laura."

But she was getting to her feet. "I'm going to dive from the bridge."

"Why do that?"

"Because."

Spilling the towel from her shoulders, shaking her head, pulling the bathing-cap on, presenting to him her ample back and walking off, not once giving him a glance.

"Laura, you're not serious."

"I do it all the time. The kids gasp."

Thinking about that and calling the thought. "You hear them gasp? Before or after they scrape you up?" But that was cruel. "I'd much rather you didn't, Laura, not if I've got anything to do with it."

He was on his feet, agitated, and she was squeezing through the wire that fenced the railway land off. "I'll go away, Laura. I'll be gone if it's me you're trying to impress."

Suddenly looking back at him. "I said I do it all the time. It's nothing. Don't you go away. Don't you be mean. You make sure you watch."

"I don't want to watch. It's stupid. It's too high. Holy cow, Laura, you'll break your neck."

"I've never broken it before."

"What if a train comes through?"

"The train's gone. It goes at twenty to eight and doesn't come back till tonight."

She can't mean it, Josh. Why would the silly-looking girl risk her life?

Laura leaving the fence behind, elbowing into scrub and tall grass towards the embankment, so feminine, arms bent, hands so graceful.

"Snakes, Laura. Snakes in the grass. You haven't got your shoes on."

"Don't be a sonk."

Josh found himself taking very strong exception to that and went pacing after her to the fence.

"Come back."

"I won't. You make sure you watch. I can do it. I do it all the time."

"Only boys do crazy things like that." Banging his forearms against the top strand of wire. "I'll tell your mother."

"I haven't got a mother."

Josh could have bitten into his tongue. Aunt Clara had not told him *that*! Hit for six. How could he shout abuse at a girl on top of that?

Aunt Clara, you've sold me short. We were talking last night. I thought you'd given me the history of every Ryan Creek family back to Noah's ark.

"Laura, don't be a fool."

Climbing the embankment on her way to the top. Josh plunging through the wire after her, but that stupid haversack was still on his back and it got hooked, tugging backwards and forwards, hooked like a fish, hurting himself.

"What's the use! If she's going to kill herself she's going to kill herself."

Giving up. Taking things quietly. Working his arms out through the straps and wriggling back through the wires to the outside of the fence, the stupid pack dropping at his feet. Josh Plowman, you can't take a trick.

"Laura, will you come down from there at once. I don't care if you do the dive every day of the week."

Picking her way along the top, beside the rails no doubt, looking down at him, shouting, "You watch."

"Laura Jones, you're completely cracked."

"You won't see from there. Go back, go back. Back to the dam. Don't spoil it for me, Josh."

How did you get through to her? It was like appealing to the better judgement of a rock.

"Go on. Go back. Please, Josh."

"Laura, I refuse to believe you make a habit of jumping off that thing."

"You're not daring me to prove it?"

"No, I'm not. And don't you try to put that on me. I thought you had more sense."

"I do it all the time, Josh. It's nothing."

"Well, if it's nothing, why do you want me to watch?"

Standing up there, away up there, silly silly girl, and suddenly walking on again, on along the embankment and gingerly on to the bridge. Picking her way. No hand rail. No parapet. Just logs trimmed square long ago and a sheer drop.

"Please, Josh, come over where you can see."

"I can see more than enough from here."

"But not when I hit the water. I want you to see me then. Don't spoil it for me, Josh."

A horrible feeling that she was doing it especially for him. A conviction that she was. A dread that she was. Laura, I can read you like the page of a book. You don't have to prove anything to me. I can't help it if I think Betsy's nice. Honest to goodness, Laura, Harry was right. Any other time I wouldn't look at you twice. Why risk your neck for me? I'll be gone in a week.

"Laura, you must come down."

"No."

"I'll get Harry."

"Harry's miles away by now. And he wouldn't care."

"If Harry doesn't care he's a bigger fool than he looks."

Laura standing at the edge waiting on him to move. How deep was the water underneath? Deep enough or not? Or would she hit the trestles going down and break herself? Was there clearance enough? Could she leap far enough out? Oh, Laura, I don't believe it, I don't believe it, you've never made that jump.

Laura standing at the edge, waiting.

You've got to get her, Josh. She's simple all right. It just doesn't show all the time; she can be sly, she can be cute, but it's down underneath. How do you get mixed up with people like this? One minute it's a giggle, the next you don't know what. Has it ever been different from the day you could walk? The odd-balls and the cranks, home to your house like they had nowhere else to live. You're a natural, Josh, cursed with a kind face.

"Laura, I'm not going to watch. I'll shut my eyes. I'll shut them tight. I don't think it's clever, I think you're showing off. Now be a good girl and come down at once."

"Please, Josh."

You've got to bring her back. You're responsible, Josh; that's what you always say to Mum when you bring home another creep. You've got to look after this kid. She hasn't the wit to look after herself. Doesn't matter how old she is, fifteen, sixteen, doesn't matter what. She's only a little girl, Josh, that's what Aunt Clara meant. She should have made it plainer. Should have said, "Steer clear of that girl. When you sight her coming you run for your life." Or something like that.

"Laura, I'm coming up."

"What for?"

"Never you mind."

"Are you going to dive, too?"

"Not on your ruddy life."

Legging through the fence, pushing through grass as high as his hips. No snake stick. What do you do when you get there, Josh? Pick her up and carry her kicking back? Brother, you couldn't prise her off the deck. Pick her up and you'd sink through solid earth, out of sight.

"You're coming up here to stop me, aren't you?"

"I wouldn't say that."

"To have a better look?"

"Could be."

It's keeping her talking at least.

"If you can't stand heights, Josh, you'll fall off."

"I'm not reckoning on falling, Laura."

"Last fellow who fell got killed."

"Doesn't surprise me in the least."

"Landed on his head. I'd rather you didn't come. I don't want you to get hurt."

Holy cow! Listen to that!

Scrambling up the embankment but repeatedly slipping back. She sailed up barefoot, but by golly, Josh, you're labouring a bit. Maybe it *is* a habit of hers. Practice makes perfect and all that. You're going to look a proper twit if she does climb it once a day and daily makes the leap and you can't even get to the top. Charging it. Talk about Don Quixote and a windmill knocking him fiat. Talk about Josh Plowman of the tender feet not game to take off his boots. Toenails not cut. Hole in sock. Most unPlowmanlike.

Half-way up, more or less, breaking out in a hot sweat, slipping and slithering and hanging to a wattle bush, Laura calling from the bridge. "It's railway property inside the fence. If the station-master sees you he'll tell your Auntie."

Panting and muttering under his breath, the humiliation almost too much.

"Can you see the dam from there, Josh?"

"Yeh."

"All right! Watch!"

Jumping Jehosaphat.

"*Laura. Don't.*"

Arching out with a tremendous leap, not diving at all, squatting in mid air, one hand held high, the other to her nostrils pinching

them shut. Dropping like a ton of bricks, flashing between the trestles. An incredible terrible splash. Josh falling too, slithering wildly
down the slope, screaming, "She'll be dead." Crashing through
the scrub, running flat out. "You ratbag, Laura Jones!" Suddenly
thinking of the wire fence, a reflex thought, like an explosion in
his brain, but too late. A horrible collision, twanging wires and
flailing limbs, Josh on his head, every breath in his body expelled
into the earth.

Lying there stupid, three parts stunned, crying inside out of pity
for himself. You poor body. You poor thing. You'll never, never
see twenty-one. How do you put up with it? Always getting hurt,
always getting tossed, always getting beaten like a rug.

Feeling sick in the head. Feeling sore in the head. Feeling
different there.

Brain damage, Josh. Oh my gosh. Your brilliance gone. Your
genius dead. Never write another poem as long as you live. Because
a nitwit jumps off a bridge. Think of a poem, Josh. Think hard.
Think quick. The boy stood on the burning deck with half a
sausage round his neck.

Dragging himself up on the wire, shaking from head to foot,
scared he was going to vomit all over the place, disconcerted
further to discover he was *outside* the fence and with not a sign of
Laura, not a trace. Staggering back to the dam, gasping for breath,
with a pain in his middle like a knotted rope. He'd bite her in half.
He'd kill her.

Nothing of Laura. Yellow ripples still lapping the bank. No
Laura out there. No Laura on dry ground. Her towel where she'd
dropped it, her clothes still in a heap.

Oh, Josh.

The water's too deep. You'll sink.

"Laura." Crying from the heart. "What have you done to yourself?"

You clown, Josh Plowman. You tangle-footed freak. Couldn't climb a bank. Couldn't swim to save your life. Can't stand up.

"Laura."

Floundering down to the water, boots sinking in the mud, wading out, calling for her, quickly sinking, chest-deep.

"I'm all right, Josh."

Looking for her. Where the heck? An arm, an arm reaching up to a strut in the shadow underneath, clinging to Heaven knows what, a spike or a bolt or a split in the wood.

"You can go back, Josh. I'll be all right in a minute."

"You silly girl."

"I did it, Josh."

"You could have killed yourself."

"I did it, Josh."

"You lied to me. You'd never done it before."

"Go back, Josh. I'll be all right in a minute. If you stay where you are too long, you'll stick in the mud."

"You're hurt."

"No, I'm not."

"Well, why don't you swim out?"

"I'm getting better. Please don't stand there, Josh, you'll get stuck, and I don't feel well enough to pull you out. I did it, Josh."

"Yes, Laura."

Wrenching free his feet, wondering whether he had lost his boots, then wading back to dry land.

Godfathers, Josh. What do you make of this?

Groping up the bank, squelching, sitting heavily down, and stretching flat on his back, exhausted.

18

Eyes closed, Josh on the inside moaning in his soul, composing a poem.

Sun pouring down, Josh on the outside steaming like a kettle, parts of him hot, parts cold, parts wet, parts dry. Like a cafeteria dinner of boiled meat and salad. Distracting thought offending his poetic despair and sternly dismissed.

Josh encouraging desperately the stirrings of liquid phrases that might clothe in glory an image of green girl, yellow mud and road, and yellow light on stubble. Nothing stirring but froth, nothing coming but bubble. It's happened, Josh, it's happened, you've spiked your genius on a wire fence.

Moaning.

"You're funny, you are."

Josh recalling with dismay that the earth was not inhabited by J. Plowman entirely.

Laura beside him running a comb through her hair, towel over her shoulders, grubby-looking towel streaked with mud. Like waking up glumly thinking it is examination day, but remembering that exams were yesterday and you've failed with dismal distinction already.

"'Struth, Laura."

How long had she stayed in the water? How long had she been out of it?

"Will you hold my hand again now?"

Josh trying to pull himself together, trying not to be cruel.

"No, Laura. ..."

"You're a stinker, aren't you?"

Nodding.

"You'd better get out of those wet clothes."

Wishing she'd go away. Dreading a fresh exchange with her. Dreading trying to understand it all, though he knew that in her company he grew to something like a man.

"Your clothes. You're soaked. You'll have to get out of them."

Groaning a silent, hopeless plea for solitude and sitting up and shaking his head. "I'm all right. The sun's hot."

"You'd better loosen your boots. They might shrink." Allowing himself to be talked into that, but leaning forward made his head spin.

"Take your boots off, why don't you?"

"Don't nag. They stay on."

"Do your feet smell?"

"Not notably."

"Harry's feet smell."

Josh grimacing. "I can believe it."

"You've cut your face."

"I'll survive."

"How'd you do it?"

"Trying to get to you in a hurry. Thinking you were dead."

"Would you have cared?"

"Of course I'd have cared."

"Like you cared for the rabbit?"

Josh allowing that to pass, but she seemed only to be dreaming across the water. "No one's ever done it. Betsy's never done it."

"I'm sure she hasn't!"

"Only Brendan O'Halloran."

"Who's he?"

"He was nineteen."

"What happened to Brendan?"

"Got killed jumping off the bridge."

Josh closing his eyes, dozens of cold hands inside him. "Why did you lie to me? What a silly lie."

"I did it. You saw me."

"You were a fool."

"Miss Plowman says that if you call your brother a fool—"

"All right! I'm sorry. But you were very unwise."

"For doing something no one's done before? For doing something they can't tell me I didn't do?"

"Yes."

"For doing it and still being alive?"

Groaning. "Forget it, will you! Let's forget it. I want to be left alone, Laura. Go and play with your dolls."

Hoping for once that kids might come along. This enormous bush, this huge country, this vast sky as empty as it was when Great-grandfather Plowman came hacking his way through to the end of the rainbow. If he had found Laura waiting at the foot of it he'd have turned right round and hacked his way out again. Great-grandfather had it easy.

"What's in your lunch-bag?"

She was still there.

"Lunch."

"Enough for both of us?"

"Look, Laura, how can you think of food?"

"I'm hungry. It's hours since breakfast. I had it at half past six."

"What the heck did you have it then for?"

"So Dad could go to work."

"At that hour of the morning?"

"He delivers the bread. All around. Miles and miles and miles. Takes all day. The horse gets tired. Then I milk the cow and scald the milk and start the housework."

"What's Harry up to while you're doing all this?"

"Feeding the pigs. Seeing to the chooks. Picking the vegetables for dinner. Emptying the lavatory pan if it's the day."

Josh feeling weak. "Harry emptying what?"

"Won't empty itself."

Talk about a living death.

"Harry's clever. Harry still goes to school. He's got to do some-thing to pay his way."

"What's wrong with your father?"

"Nothing."

"Why doesn't he empty it?"

"When he's delivering the bread?"

I can't stand much more of this, Laura Jones.

"What about some lunch, Josh?"

"Oh, Laura, have a heart. Your stomach must be lined with tin."

"Aren't you going to share?"

"I didn't say that. ..." Then thinking of Harry being clever and of Laura being somewhat less. "If Harry's still going to school, Laura, what about you?"

"Why would I go to school? What for?"

Yes, Miss Jones, a very good question. "So you go to work?"

"Doing what?"

"I don't know, Laura. I'm asking you."

"Where would I go to work? Nothing round here for the likes of me. They only have the smart girls in the shops. Go to Ballarat? Is that what you mean? What's the good of going there? Cost as much on the train as I'd earn every day."

"What do you do then? Sit around?"

"Of course not."

"Isn't there something you should be doing right now?"

"Like what?"

It's a battle, Josh, and you're losing by a street.

"I was putting the question to you, Laura."

"Like having my lunch, I suppose, and helping to get the dinner ready and on Tuesday scrubbing Miss Plowman's floors."

"So you do get paid for something. You have got a job."

"What job?"

"Holy cow, Laura. Aunt Clara's floors."

"Take money from your auntie? Take money from her? What do you think I am?"

"I don't know what I think, Laura. I'm getting that way I can't think at all. Why shouldn't she pay you? Why not?"

"Take money from your auntie?"

"Yeh, yeh, if you give her honest work she can give you honest pay. It happens all over the world. Scrubbing those floors must take all day."

"Take money from your auntie?"

Drop it, Josh. Give her some lunch. Fill her up and keep her quiet. Feed her till she burbles, then she might drop off to sleep.

Holiday at Ryan Creek. Syllabus for Monday: encounter with Miss Laura Jones. Syllabus for the rest of the week? Repeat like hiccups, though for hiccups you can only blame yourself.

Whipping open the haversack, spilling out the lunch, mangled-looking packages and a bottle of lemon squash, incredibly still intact.

"It's a bit of a mess."

"Laura, if you'd been jumped on as much you'd be a physical wreck."

Unwrapping the packages with prickling discomfort. He would have been happier, much happier, hastily wrapping them up. (Aunt

Clara, what have you done to me? Aunt Clara, you're a louse. A lunch like this to eat in front of other kids?) Wholemeal bread, stale not fresh, with vegetable extract laid on thick and black. Great hunks of cheese and clumps of lettuce leaves. Carrots, baby carrots, pulled from the garden, scrubbed and bunched. A jar with a spoon, a jar of gummy stuff; obviously malt with a cod-liver taste. And honey cake, crumbled and crushed.

Laura scratching her leg, thinking about it. "Peculiar sort of lunch."

Which expressed Josh's own feelings more moderately than he felt. "What's peculiar about it?"

"What's not?"

"Come off it, Laura."

"Are you a donkey? That's what donkeys eat."

"Funny girl."

"Or a rabbit? Was it your little brother in the trap?"

"Very funny. Very funny. It's a highly nutritious lunch."

"I'm glad about that."

"Are you?"

"Well, it doesn't look good for anything else."

"Do you want it or don't you?"

"Are *you* going to eat it?"

"Of course."

"Do you always eat lunches like that?"

"Doesn't everyone?"

Laura scratching at her leg so hard she was lucky not to draw blood. "Then I'll watch."

"Do you mean I've opened this lunch, got it all unwrapped when I wasn't hungry myself, and now you reckon you'll watch?"

"That's right."

"How rotten can you get?"

"You can come home to my place if you like and I'll get you

something decent to eat. You eat that stuff and you'll neigh like a horse."

"You're a real comedienne, when you get warmed up."

"Well, are you coming home or aren't you?"

Josh thinking cunning thoughts. "Yeh, you go on ahead and get it ready. I'll be there at twelve o'clock."

Watching her brain tick over; watching her work it out. "I think you'd better come with me now."

"No, Laura."

"Why not?"

"I want to dry my clothes first."

"You've had plenty of time to do that."

"While you were here?"

Laura, also, thought about that. "I make lovely pancakes. I put herbs in them and we have them with tomato sauce. I make lots and lots. Would you like four? Harry has four as big as his plate."

"Whatever you say, Laura."

Hesitantly pulling on her dress over her swimming-costume and slipping her feet into sandals, worrying, troubled all the time. "You will come, won't you?"

"I'll come."

"I've never had a boy come to lunch. Or to tea. I never dreamt that when it happened it would be a boy like you."

Please, Laura, don't make it harder..

"They'll be lovely pancakes, Josh, you'll see. You know where I live?"

"Of course. Between Uncle Geoffrey's house and the drapery shop."

"That's *Betsy's* house."

Spitting it out. If she had been a cat her fur would have stood on end. You've done it now, Josh.

"You'd better come with me!"

"Look, Laura, just tell me where you live."

"You know the bakehouse?"

"I'll find it."

"Opposite, across the street. The gate's got a name on it. Smith."

"I thought your name was Jones."

"So it is, but that's the name on the gate. You'll come."

"Yes, Laura."

"How will you know when it's twelve o'clock?"

"I'll listen for the chimes."

"What chimes?"

"Run along, Laura. I'll be there."

"It might be twelve o'clock now."

"It's not, Laura. It couldn't be."

"You won't let me down?"

"No!" Getting mad. "But if you don't go soon I'll never get my clothes dry, and I'm not going to sit at your table sopping wet."

Laura backing off; looking hurt, looking uncertain. Poor little Laura. Poor big girl. Laura not sure at all. Looking up to the bridge, slowly raising her eyes. "I did it. I did it. And when you come it'll be my very best day." Then walking away.

Josh subsiding in something like a heap, emotionally wrung out, wondering whether the boy he had heard was himself or someone else.

"My gosh. My gosh."

Laura walking away up the track, turning every now and then perhaps to make sure he was real and was still really there. Then she walked out of sight.

"Oh my gosh."

Josh Plowman, you're the lowest form of animal life. But you cannot go to that house. You cannot.

Peace and quiet. Glorious peace and quiet.

Stretching out again on his chest in the beautiful sun, a great weight gone, beautiful relief, unwinding, something that might have been a poem again stirring down deep. Shadows of thoughts that would not come into sharp relief. But they were there. Thank you, God, for mending my head. Thinking of his lunch exposed to the sun. What the heck. Let it cook. Aunt Clara, that wasn't fair of you. I'd have eaten it at your table to make you feel good, but how could I eat food for donkeys with kids looking on?

Rolling onto his back to expose the face of his clothes to the heat. It would be better of course to take them off. You do feel gruesome, Josh. Take them off and turn them inside-out. Let the sun dry you underneath. Too much trouble. Beautiful heat. Beautiful drifting off; deeper down deep, where the stirrings of the poem are cosy and rich.

She's gone, she's gone, she's gone.

God is beautiful, God is just. ...

Aunt Clara herself said that, though maybe she'd not meant it quite like this.

19

The time would be what? Time to take himself out of the oven or turn down the heat. Gosh, Josh, you're cooked. Baste with one bottle of lemon squash.

Sitting up dizzily, swimming in sweat. The sun past overhead, past the mark, beginning the descent. Time, say, one o'clock. How long have you slept?

Where's the lemon squash? In the sun, by gosh. Hot enough to ease a cold in the head on a winter's night. A swear-word would be in order, Josh, but you can't swear over squash that Aunt Clara bottled up. Pulling out the cork with his teeth. Bitter and hot, fresh crushed fruit, almost choking himself.

Little monster with red hair and large blue eyes squatting, legs crossed, two short paces off; liquorice smears on his face.

"Is it nice, Josh?"

Josh, shamed again, blinking in the heat, lemon squash spilling from his chin and dribbling down his chest.

"You!" Sounding as if he could take to the monster with an axe.

"Hullo, Josh."

"What are you doing here? Isn't the world big enough?"

"The liquorice strap was nice. I'm thirsty now."

"Well, go home to your mother and ask her for a drink."

"I'd like some lemon, I would."

"You won't be getting any."

"I like lemon, I do."

"So do I, Sonny."

"Is that your lunch?"

"Yes!" Very sharply said.

"You've left it in the sun for the flies to get at. You've spoilt your lunch, you have. I'll tell your auntie. She'll be cross."

"You're a nice little boy, aren't you?" Josh with gravel in his voice and violence in his heart.

"I like lemon, I do."

Josh showing his teeth. "If you like it as much as all that I suppose you'd better have some." Handing it across. "Just a share, Sonny! No more!"

Sonny wiping the mouth of the bottle in his dirty palm, then drinking with practised skill, huge bubbles billowing in the bottle, Josh shouting, "Enough."

Sonny licking his lips, belching and sneezing twice down the neck of the bottle. "It's nasty and hot."

"You didn't have to drink it. Give it back."

"I'm thirsty. I've been sitting in the sun."

Josh groaning. Sonny drinking the lot. "Ta, Josh."

"Ta, my foot."

Sonny mopping his face on the back of a dirty arm. "You'll be late."

"Late? For what?"

"For pancakes at Laura's place."

"Holy cow. What do you know about that?"

Sonny sniffing and closely inspecting a rusty jam-tin made into a little bucket with a loop of wire. "Got some tadpoles I have. The yabbies wouldn't bite."

"What do you know about pancakes at Laura's place?"

"She sent me to check up."

"Did she? Well, you've checked."

"You were supposed to be there at twelve o'clock."

"It's not twelve o'clock yet."

"Yes it is. It's way past that. But I knew you didn't want to go, so I didn't wake you up."

Josh saying nothing, not to a dangerous one like that. "I might see Laura this afternoon. I might tell her you said she could jump in the creek."

"Don't you dare!"

"I'd like a chocolate frog, I would."

"All you'll be getting from me is a thick ear."

"If I had a penny I could go to the lolly shop, and I wouldn't have to go to Laura's place."

"I haven't got a penny."

"You could look."

"Do you think I'm a millionaire or something?"

"I could tell Laura you said she was ugly."

"You wouldn't!"

"I could tell Harry you stood his sister up because she's fat."

Josh staring. Josh unable to believe his ears. "You little flea. And yesterday you carried Aunt Clara's books. You sang hymns. You took up the collection. How much did you take out of the plate for yourself?"

"I could tell Harry you said that. Harry's my cousin, he is. Harry lives next door to me he does. I could tell my Dad too. My Dad's friend is a policeman in Ballarat."

"By golly, Sonny, I bet the only policeman your Dad knows is the one he meets when he gets locked up. By golly, I'd like to call your bluff."

Sonny peering into his rusty jam-tin, maintaining silence, not understanding perhaps, or else testing the threat. Holy cow, Josh, what do you do with a monster like this?

"All right! You can have my lunch."

"If I ate your lunch, your auntie would get to hear of it, I think."

"You horrible little crook. I hope I'm not around when you grow up. I've got a pencil. Will that do?"

"I've got three pencils. I'd rather have a chocolate frog."

"If I give you another penny it's the last. The very, very, final last. If you come blackmailing me again I'll shake you till you rattle." Josh hunting for a penny. "I'll be broke. I'll have nothing to spend for the rest of the week. You go home and tell your mother to drown you." But not being able to find a penny. Jumping Jehosaphat. He had lost his money!

"I want my penny."

Snarling. "There isn't any penny."

"I'll tell."

Josh exploding. "You do that. You tell who you like. You tell what you like. I couldn't care less. There isn't any penny. There isn't any money. I've lost it! All my money. Lost it!"

"I want my penny."

"I'll flatten you, Sonny."

"I want my penny.

"I'm warning you—"

"You wouldn't touch me. You wouldn't hit me. I'll tell my Mummy, I'll tell my Daddy." Backing off. Looking like Laura when she backed off. Looking worried, looking uncertain. Suddenly turning and running. "I'll tell my Mummy, I'll tell my Daddy." Crying as he ran, wailing, his rusty jam-tin left behind him.

Money, money, money. Where had he dropped it? In the bush running from the rabbit? On the embankment? Getting through the fence or falling over the top of it? At the bottom of the dam?

Sonny wailing into the distance, screaming blue murder.

20

Josh Plowman heading for the yellow stubble, for the yellow horizon, for the wide-open plains where men died of thirst and privation if they were lucky. Or got lost and prayed no one would find them. The finger-post said, *Melbourne* 110 *mls*. What an extraordinary direction. Out the other way it was only ninety-five. Limping along with a new stick of wattle, empty pack flopping on his shoulders, empty pocket where there should have been money, biting at withered-up baby carrots. Thinking of Aunt Clara. Thinking of Laura. Thinking of Sonny. Thinking up explanations for the note they'd find beside the body.

I don't know how it happened, Aunt Clara. I guess it's my natural talent for getting into trouble. One thing led to another. Doesn't it always? If trouble's around I always seem to find it, but I can't find my money. Look at my fingernails. Worn ragged. Scratching in the dirt looking for pennies. Four weeks' hard labour. Lining tennis courts on Saturday mornings. Mowing lawns on Sundays. Saving up the surplus. I bet if the little monster comes back he'll find it in an instant.

I'm sorry about that, Aunt Clara, but I didn't know he'd go home screaming. I didn't lay a hand on him, honest, but if I'd got him by the throat I'd have killed him. Horrid little blackmailer, I'll bet he's loaded. Pennies in the mattress, pennies under the floor-boards, pennies down the garden. Lock up your silver, Aunt Clara,

he's studying to be a criminal. You'll have to tell him different
stories. No more Egyptians getting slaughtered. If God can knock
off heads he reckons he can make a penny. Living out in the sun?
Every kid in town must be paying for protection.

This business with Laura. You've got to understand it, Aunt
Clara. She's predatory. You weren't there, you wouldn't credit
it. What with her and Sonny, this town's not safe for people. I
wouldn't have gone home to her house to help fight a fire. If she's
tearing her hair, that's too bad. If she's shouting it from the house-
tops, I couldn't care. If she's hung herself from the chandelier, send
some flowers. Let her get her hooks in me? I'd never have got them
out again. I'm only a little boy, I don't want to get married.

I don't care what they tell you, Aunt Clara. I don't care. I don't
care. I don't know how it happened; it was there; and I was passing
through. If it's going to happen it happens, and if you're there
you're in it.

Plodding into the yellow distance talking to the birds. Crows.
Squawking black crows. For picking clean the bones. Go away,
you vulturous horrors. Go and find a body some other place. Can't
you see I'm breathing?

Like history, Aunt Clara. Like the war. It was there. That fellow
who came to school and leant on a stick talked about the war. Had
us in fits. Afterwards, he said, you've got to laugh, though you're not
exactly laughing fit to kill yourself at the time. Afterwards, he said, it
always looks as if the human tragedy is played by clowns. I'm working
on that one, Aunt Clara, and it's getting plainer by the hour. He never
told us how it left him bent. Never told us how he nearly died. I read
that in a book by someone else, a regimental history, that Mum dug
up at the library. All the things were there, Aunt Clara, all the things
he said, but all so deadly serious, no one cracking a grin. Everyone
being a hero but all like lumps of wood. No one doing a quiver. No
one wetting his pants. Laughing, he said, is the way of a man.

What are you doing, Josh?

Laughing.

With a face as long as a kite?

"I'm laughing!"

Hate to see you crying, boy.

Josh sitting himself on a rock, chin in hand, puffing flies from his eyes.

Little Laura Jones, what have I done to you? Aunt Clara might understand, but you never will. You recited your poem for me, jumped off a bridge for me, risked your life for me, made pancakes for me, and I treated you like dirt.

I'm crying for her. No tears, but crying.

21

In the distance a far-away squeak heard on the breeze from the south. A man with a horse and cart as if in miniature on a huge landscape, painted in as an afterthought, minute by minute growing larger as if determined to change the landscape to portrait of man, cart and horse.

Josh toying with that thought, Josh twisting it about. Poets greater than Josh had written of less. Josh plodding towards the picture; man, cart and horse squeaking out of it.

Horse with a hat, ears poking up. Lay your ears flat, horse, then the squeak may not hurt. Flat-trayed cart with man sitting high on a box. Put a cushion there, man, then the box will be soft. Hay bundles on the cart jolting about. Bale yourself hay, and you won't fall off. Boys riding near the back, legs swinging from the edge. Put your hands under your knees, then the edge won't chafe.

Josh standing aside to let the cart pass.

"You're heading the wrong way. The shooting's all done. Jump up."

The cart had stopped and the man was looking down and the boys had no need to turn their heads.

"I'm Mitchell, friend of your aunt's. You met me at church. I thought I'd see you today. What happened?"

Oh, Josh, you should have seen, you should have guessed.

"Nothing happened, Mr. Mitchell. I didn't make it, that's all."

"Some other time, eh?"

"Yes, sir."

"Jump up, Josh. Tons of room. I'll run you home."

"I'm not actually ready to go home, sir. I'm not expected till four."

"You'd better hurry then. It's already after five."

"It's *not*!"

"It is. Jump up."

Josh walking down the side looking for a hole in the hay. No hole, except next to Harry, Bill and Rex, Harry offering a hand to pull him up, Josh not wanting to take it but having to because the man had eyes to follow him and a frown on his face. Laying his wattle stick along the edge, grabbing the hand which unnecessarily crushed his knuckles and scrambling up.

"Thank you, Mr. Mitchell, I'm all right."

"Giddee-ap!"

Jerking with the cart, flinching from the squeak, wriggling into a place, aware with nauseous discomfort of three dead rabbits and a large bird with its head blown off; aware of blood on Harry's trousers and of Rex's silly grin. That kid couldn't help himself.

"What have you been doing all day?" Harry keeping his voice low, keeping it close to Josh's ear, breathing down Josh's neck.

"Nothing."

"For a doer of nothing you've got yourself in a mess."

Josh shrugging, trying to get away from the pressure of Harry's shoulder, from its unmistakable threat. Harry had changed. It was just as well there was a man up front. But Josh couldn't see him for hay. And the man would never hear above the lurching and the squeaking.

"What were you doing in the dam?"

"Did I say anything about being in the dam?"

"You don't have to say it. You smell it. What were you doing in it with your clothes on?"

"That's my business."

"With Laura being there, it's my business too."

"Laura's all right."

"Why shouldn't she be?"

Josh compressing his lips. Taking a breath. "You brought it up. I'm not her nursemaid. Laura's big enough to look after herself."

"Don't you get smart about Laura, Joshua. Laura's got to be treated right. She's not used to smart alecs."

"She was there, wasn't she? I didn't ask her to be there. If you were worried you should have sent her home."

"What'd he say?" Bill was straining to hear round the back of Rex, that stupid Rex who must have been born with a snigger on his face.

"He says he's been in the dam."

"I didn't say it. Harry said it."

"What's he been doing in the dam?"

"I don't know, but he stinks of it. She's been churning that mud up and he's been in it, boots and all."

"I told you so. You shouldn't have left her there."

"I thought he'd go home and weep on Auntie's shoulder. So did you. What's he been doing all day? It's five o'clock."

Rex giggling. "Well, he couldn't have been chasing Betsy if he's been chasing Laura."

Harry pressing against Josh. "Was Betsy there?"

"You'd better ask Betsy."

"I'm asking you."

Josh shrugging, trying to be calm, trying to give nothing away, trying to remember Dad's advice for unequal encounters: "Keep 'em guessing." But there was a limit and he was running close.

"You steer clear of our girls, Joshua. You leave them alone."

"The name is *Josh*."

"I say it's Joshua and so does your auntie. But it'll be nothin' if you don't leave those girls alone."

"I'm not interested in your girls."

"Aren't they good enough for you?"

"Oh, for Pete's sake. Look, I'm fourteen, not twenty-eight. I don't go around with girls."

"Keep your voice down! Keep your voice down!"

"If I want to shout, Harry Jones, I'll ruddy well shout. Haven't you kids got any other thought in your heads? I'm not allowed to go out with girls and I don't particularly want to."

"You were giving Betsy the eye on the train. You were ogling her in Sunday-school. You couldn't turn your head away from her out in the street."

"So what? She's pretty. She's nice to look at. That doesn't mean I want to take her out, and if I did I wouldn't ask your permission. What are you, her grandfather or something?"

"She told Bill. She said tell that creep to lay off. So I'm telling you."

"All right. You've told me. Now what?"

"Don't you go home whining to your auntie again. Don't you go home whingeing to her. All you've done since you hit this place is stir up trouble."

"I haven't whined and I haven't stirred up trouble!"

"Will you keep your voice down!"

"No, I won't. If you've got anything to hide, I haven't. I'm sick of covering up for you lot."

"You're sick of *what*?"

"I've said not one word out of place with Aunt Clara. She doesn't even know you sneer at her behind her back. I reckon you're the crummiest bunch I've met up with in my life. If we had kids like you at home you wouldn't rate a spit in the eye."

Josh's hands thrusting against the lip of the cart, leaping away, crunching in the yellow gravel on his knees.

"*Whoah*!"

The cart stopping. The three kids lined up along the side, three faces of innocence, no evil heard, no evil spoken, no evil seen. Three kids as stiff as statues and the man swinging down to the road.

"All right, what's it all about?"

Josh getting to his feet, a wild storm of nerves inside, pale and trembling and tight-lipped on the outside.

"Josh. Did you fall or were you pushed?"

Josh taking a deep breath, a very deep breath, hoping his voice when it came could be heard. "I jumped."

"That was a silly thing to do."

"I want to walk."

"When you can ride?"

"I want to walk on my own, Mr. Mitchell, thank you all the same. I'm not used to carts. It's the jolting up and down. I'm feeling sick."

"Are you?"

"Yes, sir."

The man rubbing at his neck and looking along the side, looking long at Harry, Bill and Rex, then swinging up again to his box.

"Don't drag your feet, Josh. Your aunt will be worried if it gets much later than this."

Hay cart squeaking away, Josh limping after it. Different picture now, different landscape, hay cart getting smaller and smaller, Great-grandfather's bridge a sign in the sky.

"Go away, crows. I'm still breathing."

22

Fat white George asleep on the doormat. Josh home from the wars, home, home, to wood smoke and lavender.

"Is that you, Josh?"

"Yes, Aunt Clara."

"Come into the kitchen and tell me about it."

"I think I'd better change. I'm dirty."

Swaying with uncertainty, marooned in the lobby. Home, Josh, but what tales have raced home before you? Aunt Clara now framed in the doorway stirring at a bowl with less than proper attention, stirring slower and slower.

"Are you all right, Josh?"

"Yes, thank you."

Aunt Clara's spoon poised without motion. "You're later than expected."

"It was that kind of day, Aunt Clara."

"Have you enjoyed yourself?"

"I'm not sure. I'll know better when I've thought about it."

Aunt Clara stirring again, slowly. "That's a grown-up remark. Are you a little older than you were at nine -thirty this morning?"

The doorway empty, her voice continuing from the kitchen. "The bath-heater's set and ready. Only wants a match to it. You know how to light it. Drop your clothes in the laundry. I'll bring clean ones to you."

Responding to directions like a clockwork model, not resentfully, but grateful for simple things that could be done without thinking or risk of provoking an issue.

Ryan Creek is like another country, different climate, different people, different happenings. This is like the world Dad says is waiting when you cut out from home to make your fortune. The old priorities don't mean anything. You're not the centre of the universe any longer. Life starts getting rugged.

Sitting in his underpants on a stool beside the bathtub listening to the chuffing of the heater. Bathtub big enough to drown in, on feet like an elephant's, great shelf of mahogany for flowers and toiletries, tiles on the floor imported from Italy, ferns and ivys and curious succulents spilling from baskets hanging from the ceiling, sun streaming past the open window-sashes, everything steamy, Aunt Clara there, Josh sensing her presence.

"Aunt Clara, is there a special reason why you don't pay Laura?"

Josh turning on the stool as if on a slow swivel, Aunt Clara perhaps suddenly laying out clothes on a low marble table.

"That's a strange question. What would you know about Laura?"

"Not much. Is she simple?"

"No, Josh, I'd not call her simple in the way I think you mean it. Certainly I'd not. Who's been talking about Laura?"

Perhaps it would have been better not to have started it. Start anything and where's it going to finish? Turn a stone and what's underneath it? Ask a question and get another back at you. Sitting there silent almost scared to make a comment, Aunt Clara waiting.

"It was a very funny day, Aunt Clara."

"You spent a lot of time laughing?"

"No, I didn't, but I spent some of the time trying."

"How was the shooting?"

Josh, you're a devil for punishment. You've made the mistake and now you're for it. You should have buttoned up your lip and said nothing.

"I don't think I go much for killing, Aunt Clara."

"Country people don't regard it … as killing."

"I don't know how anyone could regard it as not killing."

Aunt Clara looking sad, or was that imagination? She's ahead of you, Josh; much too old and much too wise for a kid who cries for a rabbit.

"And was that all that troubled you?"

"I said it was a very funny day, Aunt Clara."

"But you don't want to tell me?"

"Do I have to?"

"There's no compulsion."

Sighing. "Haven't you heard already?"

"What could I hear, Josh, unless you tell me?"

She's not answering. She's staying ahead. And what makes it worse, you know it. Oh, Josh, turn back the clock, turn it back a minute, and sit there silent saying nothing.

"Look, Aunt Clara, can't we come clean.? I know they've told you."

"Who might *they* be? Haven't you been shooting? Weren't you at Mitchell's?"

"Hasn't Sonny been to see you?"

"Who's Sonny? Every male in town will answer to Sonny, except the oldest inhabitant."

"Little red-haired kid." Josh swallowing. "He carried your books to Sunday-school."

"Was he bringing something?"

Josh shaking his head, for the moment a useful gesture; it seemed to cover everything.

"The bath-heater, Josh. Do put some chips on it. You'll need more than a puddle to wash in. And in answer to your first question, yes, there is a reason why I do not pay Laura, but it's nothing that should worry you, and you are worried or you wouldn't have asked me. What's your interest in Laura? I thought your interest was Betsy."

"I haven't said anything about Betsy."

Aunt Clara smiling. "No, Josh, you haven't. Betsy's a good girl. I like her."

"But you don't like Laura?"

"Goodness, Josh, that's a rash conclusion on so little evidence. I'm especially fond of Laura."

"Well, why didn't you tell me she didn't have a mother?"

"Laura? I was not under the impression she was going to Mitchell's with you."

"She didn't."

"Josh, one thing about our Laura. ...

Aunt Clara going silent, Aunt Clara looking anxious, Josh's dismay leaping upwards. "She wouldn't lie about her mother!"

"Laura has a mother."

"At home? Looking after her?"

"At home, Josh, looking after her."

Oh, Laura. Oh, Laura Jones.

"Josh, is there anything in particular you want to tell me?"

"No, Aunt Clara."

"There's nothing troubling you uncommonly?"

"Nothing that's going to get easier by talking about it. ... I saw the bridge, Aunt Clara."

"Josh, we don't solve problems by shutting a door on them."

"Please, Aunt Clara, can't we shut this one? Great-grandfather's bridge was wonderful."

"He would be happy to hear you say it. He made good use

of local materials and used them honestly. The world is full of beautiful bridges and beautiful poems, each stating a solution to a problem. A bridge is a very noble structure. The ones I marvel at were built by the ancients."

"I like Great-grandfather's."

Aunt Clara smiling. "It's a good thing to have in the family. On Wednesday, Josh, I think we'll catch the train and go to Ballarat. A special Plowman excursion. So in the meantime don't spend all your money on ice-cream and peanuts."

"It's a bit late for that, Aunt Clara."

"Aren't you interested?"

"I've lost my money."

Josh looking at the floor, at the pattern on the tiles.

"Well, you must make an effort to find it."

"I have made an effort, Aunt Clara. But it's only money."

"My goodness, Josh, you never cease to surprise me. You're a young head to make that admission."

Josh shrugging.

"Where did you lose it?"

"If I knew for certain, I think I might have found it."

Still avoiding her, still staring at the tiles.

"Honest money, Josh, is not an evil, even if you have discovered other things more important. What time is cricket?"

Josh glancing up, startled.

"When do you have to be there? You're playing, aren't you?"

"I don't know."

"You enjoy cricket, don't you?"

"Yes, Aunt Clara."

"Well, first thing in the morning you'd better get across to Bill and ask him. You know, I believe you're as absent-minded as your Great-grandfather. Keeping him out of trouble was quite an undertaking. He used to enter his engagements meticulously in his diary, then forgot to refer to it."

She was looking at him with intensity, making him feel extremely self-conscious.

"You're big-boned, rather like him. But he was never heavy although he looked it. Josh, don't forget Ballarat on Wednesday. We can buy your Bible and have lunch in the gardens and visit the museum. There are relics there of Great-grandfather. Things of special interest to the Plowmans that the museum accepted from me. He was a good man, my father. He believed in people. It often left him hurt and got him into difficulties, but he went on believing in people."

Josh soaking in the bath, alone with mysteries.

TUESDAY

23

Josh down on one knee at the edge of the gutter outside Uncle Geoffrey's house on the High Street, poor old house behind the fence looking forlorn with its shutters up, lying there empty. Why didn't someone rent it? Was it haunted? Josh nervously fiddling with a bootlace, putting on an act, pretending to tighten it, pretending not to be able to adjust it comfortably.

Gosh, Josh, life sure is wearing.

That wide street full of morning eyes, the picket fences and the shop-fronts, the early birds at the post-office steps waiting for nine o'clock. What would anyone want in a post-office at nine o'clock? A kid on a bicycle peering at him as he rode past, wobbling, nearly falling off; a girl leading a cow on a rope, a huge fat cow, poor waddling mummy, they should have loaded her on a truck and carried her to the dairy.

Josh tightening his pretending bootlace until any mortal foot should have cracked.

It was easy for Aunt Clara. She had no idea what lay behind it. "Run across to Bill's, Josh. Why are you so reluctant? It won't take a minute. Perhaps you'd have done better to have gone last evening."

Gosh, Aunt Clara, this living on two fronts is tearing me to tatters.

The O'Connor house where Bill lived and Rex lived and Betsy

lived, not a hundred yards from gate to gate. There in a minute! If it had been a mile or ten miles, then there'd have been an excuse he could have given her. Next to Uncle Geoffrey's house. Much too close for comfort.

Josh releasing his pretending bootlace, as if he'd got it tangled, pretending to tighten it again, pretending, pretending, staving off the inevitable.

I mean, Josh, the cheek of it!

The nerve of knocking on that door, of standing there, of asking, "Hi, Bill, what about the cricket match? Where you going to play me, Bill? When's it going to start?"

He couldn't, he couldn't stand up to Bill with that kind of effrontery, and he couldn't go back to Aunt Clara unless he did. Perhaps another approach, cap in hand, looking sheepish. "It's this way, Bill, I know it's a cheek, but Aunt Clara sent me over. She wants an answer about the cricket match." Bill would blow his top. Then there'd be the going back to Aunt Clara, trying to dress it up. "Bill's got his team. It was too late. I'm sorry, Aunt Clara, but he hasn't seen me play and couldn't take the risk. I know you wanted me to play, a Plowman in the team and all that, I know you wanted to come and watch. I'm disappointed too, but Bill's right. He's got to put his team first."

Oh golly gosh.

Josh straightening up. If he messed about with that pretending bootlace one more instant, everyone in the street would think he was a nut.

Uncle Geoffrey's house still behind the fence, the O'Connor house still next door, path waiting to be walked up. Uncle Geoffrey, God rest him, in the graveyard for fifteen years, dying before you had the chance to meet him, Josh. Great-grandfather six feet under for a quarter of a century. Seven Plowmans pushing up the daisies amongst the pine-trees at the back of High Street. Must visit the cemetery. Must pick a nice bunch of pansies for making into posies. No time like the present. Must go and pay my respects like a proper Plowman; should have done it Sunday. Josh, Josh, who are you kidding? Get the dirty deed done.

Making it to the O'Connor gate, hanging to it to marshal his resources, lifting the latch, walking the path to the front-door mat, stumbling on the step in the best J. Plowman manner, wanting to vanish, gripping a veranda post so he wouldn't fall over, wanting to turn and run for the horizon, stomach in a knot, wanting to belch, footsteps coming. What a life. Inner door opening.

Betsy.

Face to face with Betsy.

Eye to eye with Betsy.

Alone with Betsy; not another living human yet invented.

She's a dish. She's a stunner. Doesn't matter what she called you. Ford the river. Climb the mountains. Sing a chorus with the angels.

"Hullo, Betsy."

"What are you doing here?"

Like he was a dog who'd come to the wrong address. Like he was an onion in a tulip patch.

"What do you want?"

Dare I express myself, Miss Betsy O'Connor? Dare I risk the wrath of Harry and ask you home to lunch? This is really quite extraordinary because I'm not a boy like that. There never was a girl who wasn't a pain in the neck.

"Oh, come on. Say what you've got to say, then hop it. I'm busy."

"Betsy, don't be cross with me," scarcely believing himself because from Laura he had heard the very same entreaty.

"Is that all? Goodbye."

"Look, Betsy, the cricket match."

"Do I play cricket? Would I know about a cricket match?"

Shaking his head.

"Is it Bill you want?"

Nodding.

"You sure are a dumb kid. ... *Bill*!" Shrieking like a factory whistle. "The Plowman kid, to see you about the cricket match."

Betsy gone into the gloom beyond the screen door. Oh, Betsy. I'm not dirt to be walked on. Don't spoil yourself by being coarse.

Bill, as surly as a watchdog, not coming into the light where Josh could properly see him. "Yeh? What about the cricket match?"

"Bill!" A voice calling from inside the house. "If that's Josh Plowman invite him in. Don't leave him on the mat."

"He can't stay, Mum. He's got to rush back."

"I'm sure Miss Plowman won't mind if he spends a few minutes. Bring him in."

Bill mumbling under his breath and giving the screen door a push. "You heard, come in, but don't kid yourself, mate. There's always afterwards. You say anythin' and I'll get you."

"Anything about what?"

"About anythin'."

Gosh, Josh. Talk about an open cheque. Stepping into the cool out of the morning sun, feeling his way, scared he was going to trip, not putting it past Bill to shoot out a foot, groping along a passage like a mine shaft, house smelling of madonna lilies or ant bait. Into a kitchen with a scrubbed pine table and a wash-up dish and a heap of willow-pattern plates of the kind you swapped for tea-packet labels and a surprising woman looking younger than Mum, with her sleeves rolled up and her hands in the dish. Looking like Betsy, looking like Rex.

"Hullo, Josh." Nice wrinkles round her eyes, keen eyes not missing much, a brown woman, brown and lean from living in the sun.

"Good morning, Mrs. O'Connor. Thank you for inviting me in."

"Enjoying your holiday?"

"Yes, thank you very much."

Bill looking like he'd lost a one-pound note.

"I've heard a lot about you from your aunt, but you're taller than I guessed. You've got the Plowman face. Is she fattening you up?"

"I think she's trying to, Mrs.O'Connor."

"Betsy! The dishes! Where did Betsy go, Bill?"

"I'm here, Mum."

"Well, come all the way in. Don't be shy in your own house. Josh won't bite. Get on to your dishes while they're hot. Knives and forks first. I don't have to tell you that." Betsy fumbling with the tea-towel, altogether different, completely unlike herself.

"Sit down, Josh. Take the weight off your feet."

"I can't stay, Mrs. O'Connor." Wondering about Betsy. Feeling embarrassed for her. "I've really got to get back."

"Nonsense, nonsense. Tell your aunt it was my fault. She'll understand. The kettle's boiling, Bill. Make a fresh pot.

We've never had a poet in the house. ... Now I've made him blush. My big mouth. I'm sorry, Josh, but we're very proud—aren't we, Betsy?—having a stake in someone who'll make a name for himself. We're all hoping a little of the fame will rub off."

Betsy wailing, "Oh, *Mum*!" Bill bouncing out the back door to empty the teapot. Josh struggling for something to say, but absolutely whacked.

But was Mrs.O'Connor only warming up? "Miss Plowman's seen his poems, she's excited, and she's not the kind to boast. She's got taste, she's an educated woman, and he's a Plowman and the Plowmans belong to Ryan Creek. We'll be watching for your name, Josh. We'll be owning you. We'll be saying you're one of us."

Betsy pale and tense, not looking at anything, staring straight ahead, Bill coming back in with a face like midwinter, Josh knowing he had to say something and say it at once. "Gosh, Mrs. O'Connor … I don't know that it'll be as easy as that. Aunt Clara shouldn't have told you. She shouldn't have. Those poems were private."

"They still are. She didn't say what they were about. She was excited and couldn't keep it to herself. You mustn't be hard on her because of that. Come on, Bill, get the tea in the pot, good and strong, nice and hot. A rhyme! We're all breaking into poetry, aren't we just?"

"Oh, Mum. …" Betsy looking as if she could turn into a worm and wriggle into a crack. Bill slamming the tea caddy around; lucky it was made of tin. Josh running a temperature of about a hundred and two, burning up.

"Josh, I know I sound like a silly woman, but I'm not as silly or as tactless as you think. And people here realize that. That's why I called you in. There's a freeze in this town that's gone far enough. Don't you think so, Betsy?"

"I don't know what you're talking about, Mum."

"Don't you, Bill?"

"No, I don't."

"Rex would know, I'm sure. It's a pity he's out. You kids forget your parents were young once, not so many years back. You think we walk around with our eyes shut. You think we walk around stone-deaf. You think the little birds don't come home to roost."

Betsy talking through her teeth. "I don't know what you mean."

"If you don't, you're duller than I think. If you want to keep a secret, kids, never tell the birds. Little birds come home to roost."

Bill getting darker than midwinter, much darker than that.

"About the cricket match, son."

"That's my business, Mum."

"Not entirely and you know it. You want the best team. I suppose Josh is playing."

Bill grimly, "I suppose. Can he keep wickets?"

"Don't ask me. Ask him."

"Are you any good behind the stumps?"

Josh not caring too much for the sound of that. "I thought you needed a batsman."

"Yeh, we do. One who can wicket-keep as well. The one we've got's too little."

"I can try."

In one way Bill was like his Mum. His eyes didn't miss much. Josh saw the glint.

"If you'll be wicket-keeper you can play."

"I'll play."

"Half past twelve at the recreation ground. You know where it is?"

"He doesn't have to know, Bill. He can go along with you."

"All right. Meet me here at a quarter past. Wear your whites."

"I've got a white shirt."

"That won't do. White strides, white boots, the lot. If you don't wear white, you don't play."

Josh's voice, unfortunately, turning a bit thin. "I haven't got cricket things with me."

"That's the rule. White. It's a proper match, Joshua. Not a bunch of kids fooling about. We play by the rules. All of them."

"I think his name is Josh and I think by now you know it!"

Bill glancing at his mother, trying not to look savage. "He's still got to wear whites."

"All right, Bill. If you want him to play—"

"Did I ever say that?"

"Enough of it. Don't be unkind. This isn't like you. It's up to us to find the clothes for him. You can try the Duncans and the Priors—the boys are still away—or get on your bike and push out to Hood's. Someone's clothes will have to fit. Now pour the tea."

Betsy drying dishes again with exaggerated care, slowly stacking them to one side. Betsy concentrating on her hands, avoiding Josh's eye. Betsy girl, what's on your mind? And give a fellow a break, Bill. What have I done that's so terribly bad? Gosh, Mrs. O'Connor, I don't know that it's going to work as you planned. They're showing you the face they've been showing to me, and when they can't hide it at home it's getting raw.

Drinking tea. What is it that gives Ryan Creek a perpetual raging thirst? Dirty great cupful and breakfast not gone an hour. Betsy drinking tea. Bill drinking tea. Mrs. O'Connor with a mug big enough to put her fist in. They'll bubble. Barrels inside them, Josh, barrels not stomachs. Bubble, bubble, bubble. Think you're a camel and store it in your hump.

Trouble is, Mrs. O'Connor, mothers don't know it all. Maybe what went when you were young doesn't go now. Maybe when you were a kid everybody was loving. Maybe little birds do come home to roost, whatever little birds are, but do little birds know why I'm crook on these kids? Do little birds know why they're ganging up on me?

Talking small talk. Prattling. Talking about the north wind blowing on Sunday. Talking about the train stopping seven times in five miles. Talking about the crystal leaves in Aunt Clara's ceiling tinkling every time he breathed.

"I hope you come again, Josh."

"Thank you, Mrs. O'Connor."

"Enjoy your cricket."

"Thank you, Mrs.O'Connor."

Josh getting pushed down the passage, Bill holding him by the arm not because he liked him.

"You've done your lot, mate. You've done it all."

"I haven't done anything."

"You tell that to the birds."

Suddenly out in the sunlight, physically pushed away, stumbling, no time to answer back at Bill, no chance to deny it. Bill simply not there.

Josh getting mad, getting madder and madder, feeling like jumping up and down, feeling like screaming at the door. "Who do you think you are, Bill O'Connor? Pushing me around. What do you think I am, Bill O'Connor? I haven't split on you, not a word." But the door was closed and Bill was gone and Josh stood silent, rubbing at his arm.

Gosh, Josh, things are getting out of hand. Wicket-keeper if you please. Every man's coconut-shy. If Bill's a fast bowler you'd better start praying for heavy rain beginning sharp at noon.

24

Walking in through the open front door as large as life. You've got to look the part even if you'd rather drop dead. Wearing a big beaming grin and giving a shout. "I'm in the team, Aunt Clara. He was only waiting for me to come like you said. Wicket-keeper, Aunt Clara, behind the stumps. Half past twelve it starts."

Pacing down the passage with big man strides, acting it out, pushing through the curtains. Bang.

On her knees with a scrubbing-brush and a bucket of foaming suds: Miss Laura Jones.

Laura peering through tresses of disordered hair, trying to blow a hole for unobstructed vision. Looking like a water spaniel, a very sad water spaniel, lost, stolen, or strayed. Josh trapped. *Save me, Aunt Clara!* Cut off from the kitchen, cut off from sanctuary, fronted by rolled-up mats standing on end and a droopy-eyed Laura and a lake of soap.

"Very good, Josh." The voice from the kitchen, from the unreachable woman. "I told you they'd be glad to play you. You know Laura, don't you?"

Know her? Do I what!

"Yes, Aunt Clara, I know Laura."

Laura saying nothing. Laura with a trembling lip. Trying to stare him out? Trying to shame him? She didn't need to try. Gosh, Laura, turn off the searchlights.

"Laura's a very good friend. She comes on Tuesdays to help me out."

"Yes, Aunt Clara."

"Every Tuesday without fail, though there are times I'm sure when she has enough to do at home. I couldn't manage without Laura."

You're laying it on a bit, Aunt Clara. You could manage this house and another like it and not raise a sweat.

"Don't step where Laura's working."

"No, Aunt Clara."

"Have you made your bed?"

"Yes, Aunt Clara."

"Swept your room?"

"Yes, Aunt Clara."

"Well, keep out of the way, there's a good boy. I can't have my girl being bothered. Go and weed the garden. Go and gather the eggs."

Hey, take a breath, Aunt Clara. Get off a fellow's back. I'm going, I'm going. Though where the heck I'm going is anybody's guess.

"It's not that I don't want you, Josh."

"Yeh, I understand." Like I understand relativity.

"You could run an errand for me. I'll be too busy to get to the shops. There's a lot I want. I'll make up a list."

"I can't get to you, Aunt Clara. I'll have to paddle in the soap."

"Come to the dining-room then and I'll pass it through the hatch."

Backing out through the curtains trying to avoid the sad-eyed look, trying not to notice her lips and the words they seemed to make, "*You didn't come.*"

Well, you did push it hard, Laura; fellows don't like being pushed.

Groping into the dining-room feeling cheap, astonished it had never crossed his mind that he might encounter Laura more than once. Laura with a scrubbing-brush, down on her knees, Laura working but not getting paid. Something about it was sad. The Laura who leapt from the bridge. That took—spirit.

Aunt Clara's face at the servery hatch. "The list is in the purse and the purse is in the basket. You don't mind, do you?"

"No, Aunt Clara."

"I didn't think you would. It's a big list. If you're not back until eleven it'll still be time enough."

Gosh, Josh. That was sudden.

Heading back to the street, passing through the portals of painted glass, mounting the scaffold of fifteen steps, then standing in the blazing sun scratching himself.

Ever had a funny feeling, Josh, that something's missed a beat?

Opening the purse. Nothing in it except a threepenny bit and a corner of paper ripped from a larger sheet. Marks on it scrawled in haste. "Buy yourself an ice-cream. Take a walk. God bless."

Aunt Clara, you're my mate.

25

Josh sitting on a tombstone in the Plowman plot of earth. Sitting on Great-grandfather, which seemed a very proper place.

Maximilian Plowman. Born 12.6.1821. Died 5.5.1910
Founder of Ryan Creek
He always gave his fellow man the benefit of the doubt

Gosh, Great-grandfather, I wonder who thought that up? Aunt Clara perhaps? It's nice to have it chipped in the stone they put on top of your head.

You're a hundred years older than I am, did you know that? Almost to the day. A hundred years ago and you were fourteen and seven months. What do you know about that? What was it like in 1836? Did you have somewhere in England to go to like Ryan Creek? Were you sitting on a tombstone out in the blazing sun with a silly-looking shopping-basket stuck on your head? Did you have an Aunt Clara to save you from a horrible fate? Did you have a Betsy you couldn't manage to impress? Did you have a Laura to plague your life or a Bill or a Harry or a giggling Rex? Did you have a little kid round the corner blackmailing you? What was it like then, Great-grandfather, a hundred years back?

Were you like me, everybody's football, always getting kicked?

Did you know you were going to found a town? Did you know you were going to build a bridge? Did you know you'd start a family that'd end up with Josh sitting on your tombstone paying his respects? Growing up is a funny thing, would you say that? Wondering whether you'll be famous, not dead sure you want to be or not. If you've got to go through life crying for everybody else and laughing at yourself. Was that why you painted those portraits, those crummy-looking things, because you didn't feel like laughing at anyone else?

Rosemary Caroline Plowman (née Braddock).
Born 22.3.1831. Died 14.7.1868
In loving memory of an adored wife
With God who loves her too

You had to go on forty-two years without her, Great-grandfather. You didn't have her for very long. Dead in the ground and younger than Mum. Gosh, Great-grandfather, I'm sad about that. Is that why people don't talk about her much? Dead for so long they can't remember. It's sad to be dead for so long that no one remembers. Rosemary Caroline Plowman (née Braddock). I want to put a flower here for you.

Jane Braddock Plowman. Born 14.7.1868. Lived three hours
With Jesus

Oh, golly, Great-grandfather. No one ever told me that. I'm so sad. I'm so sorry. You lost your little baby and you lost your sweetheart, too. On the same day. That's not fair. And here am I sweating about a cricket match. Did you cry, Great-grandfather? Were you a big strong man who never got upset? I'll bet you cried. I'll bet you couldn't see for tears. I do feel close; I'd like you to know that.

26

Dawdling through the tombstones swinging the basket in the shade of the pine-trees, kicking through the needles, soft as cushions, soft as feathers, not a blade of grass growing. Quiet, so quiet you can hear the sunlight falling and the shadows stirring and the earth breathing. Who planted the pines, Great-grandfather? Who planted the avenues turning the cemetery into a cathedral? Making my morning the pieces of a poem.

"Say, Joshua!"

An awful leaping feeling inside him as if something had broken loose. Harry, hands in pockets, leaning on the trunk of a pine as if he had been there an hour. Not only Harry. Rex coming round from behind, and another in the shadow he would rather not have noticed. Betsy, looking blank, like someone without intelligence. Not moving, as if pretending to herself she was in hiding.

Rex giggling, "Did your auntie tell you to go shopping in the cemetery? What have you been buying? Six feet to lie in?"

Josh wanting to run, not liking the look of it, in a way not believing it. Harry, Rex and Betsy. What did they want of him? And how many more of them were still to show their faces?

"Haven't you kids got anything better to do? Have you been following me?"

"We've been waiting." Harry pushing himself from the tree with a thrust of his shoulders. "We've got things to talk about."

"Why can't you leave me alone?"

"You're a character, aren't you?"

"Well, it's a cemetery, isn't it? I came here to be on my own."

"You weren't, kid. Rex has been keeping tags on you. About Laura."

"Look, Harry." Trying to keep his voice down to a level, trying to stop it from thinning. "What's Laura got to do with me? I told you that yesterday."

Harry rubbing his nose with the back of a large hand. "You stood her up."

Josh slumping, imagining somehow that that would have been private. Was Laura a tale-teller? But then remembering Sonny. Sonny who didn't get his penny.

"You made a promise to her and didn't keep it. Pancakes all over the house. I don't like my sister crying. I don't like my sister being made to feel a fool. Cry, cry. If it was your sister, what would you be thinking?"

"I don't know that I'd be thinking anything. I reckon I'd make sure I had more than half the story."

"Meaning Laura's a liar?"

Josh going taut again, going breathless again. "Did I say that?"

"I don't know. But didn't you?"

Glancing to Betsy, hoping for heaven knows what. Support, perhaps. Or a bit of understanding. But Betsy wasn't looking. Standing there as if she'd only brought her body along and left her sympathy somewhere else. Rex standing as if he was eight feet tall, as smug as he could get, knowing he was as strong as Harry's muscles and absolutely safe.

"I'm still waiting. Did you call Laura a liar or didn't you?"

"If that's what it sounded like, I didn't mean it. I meant *my* side of the story. There are two sides to everything."

"There's only one side to a promise. You either keep it or you don't keep it."

"Oh, leave him alone, Harry." Betsy sighing. "I told you he was dumb. He doesn't know whether it's Bourke Street or Friday. He's harmless. Laura will have to put up with it."

"*Harmless?*" Harry shrieking. "*Harmless?* He could have killed her. Laura jumping off that bridge. Him making her do it."

"Hey, wait a minute. Hey, what are you saying? That's not true."

"You mean she didn't jump off the bridge?"

Josh slumping again, slumping all over, desperately wanting not to hurt Laura, desperately trying to think of a way out of it. But Harry was so overpowering.

"And you didn't go chasing her through the wire? And you didn't go chasing her up the embankment? You listen to me kid, I've been to check, I've made sure, great slithering marks all over the place. Laura's word would be good enough, but we've got more than that for it. We've got someone who saw it from start to finish. You're lucky you got back into town last night without a thrashing. If it hadn't been for your auntie, God knows what would have happened to you. That jump killed Brendan O'Halloran and he was an athlete. Strike me, Betsy, harmless you call him? He's a lunatic And after all that he breaks his promise! Jump from the bridge, he tells her, and I'll come home for pancakes. He's twisted. Then threatens to beat up young Jimmy if he tells on him. What's wrong with him? Hasn't he got respect for anybody? Even his auntie? Egging a girl on like that. He got out of the house quick smart this morning, didn't he? Scarcely put his foot in it and out again. Great big act. Shopping-basket and no shopping. Rex saw him. Who ever took a shopping-basket to buy an ice-cream?"

Josh trying to get a word in, wailing, "Look, it's all circumstantial. I don't care how it seems, but I've done nothing. I've done nothing."

"Circumstantial?" Harry not really sneering, almost sounding tired. "Now he starts chucking big words at us. What's wrong with you Plowmans? I did try to like you, I went right out of my way to like you. For her I did it, like we all did it. But you Plowmans never alter. I don't know how she puts up with you. One after the other. You come in here thinking you own the place, strutting like turkey cocks, pushing people around, running home to auntie the minute someone pushes back."

"That's not true!"

"Look, kid, your auntie's too good to be saddled with the likes of you. All you Plowmans, one after the other, coming up here sponging on her, taking everything she's got and never giving her a 'thank you.' We know your kind; we get to hear. Everyone in town knows she's mortgaged to the eyebrows paying for the education of other people's kids, giving people houses to live in for free. Yet you Plowmans with all the loot in the world go on bleeding her, taking home a pile of stuff every time you call."

"It's not true!"

"We've had you Plowmans. We've had you right up to the ears."

"It's not true. ..." Josh fading into a feeling of sickness, bewildered by Harry. "She's rich. Anything she gives she can afford ..."

"Yeh, she's rich; she's rich all right. How do you think we feel? Knowing she's living on the smell of an oily rag. I'm telling you, kid, as far as everyone in Ryan Creek is concerned the only Plowman who's cut any ice round here for a very long time is her. Little tin gods. Thinking they own the place. And you have the nerve to stand there and say you've done nothing."

"But I *haven't*." Josh trying to sound as if he wasn't crying. "I don't know what you're talking about. It's double-Dutch to me. Nothing to do with me. I keep on saying it, *I've done nothing.*" Looking to Betsy, hoping for the miracle, that she'd not stand by watching him persecuted. Betsy was a good girl. Aunt Clara said so. Please, Betsy ...

Harry sounding tired again. "You can't talk to them, can you? He keeps on saying it, he says he's done nothing. So help me bob, what's he got to do before he reckons he's in business?"

Rex giggling and Betsy speaking up, as toneless as Harry. "What's the use? I told you. We're making too much of it. The poor drip's *non compos*."

"Making too much of it?" Harry shrilling. "Look at Laura, poor old Laura. Never had a boy in her life and goes for a crumb like this one. I'm getting him for that; I'm getting you, Joshua; I'm serving notice. Look at me! Feeling guilty for clubbing a lousy rabbit. Look at Jimmy, coming home howling. Eight years old and you send him off screaming. If your auntie hadn't stopped him his father would have brained you. Look at Betsy, having to put up with your staring every-where she goes; you leave her alone. Look at all of us, scared to meet your auntie in the eye for what you might have said to her, twisting everything around until it's like nothing we ever thought of. Oh, you're a honey, kid. You're the daddy of all the Plowmans and that's saying something. And then you've got the hide to corner Bill in front of his mother and ask about *cricket*. Bill, having to gallivant all over the country, begging for clothes for you to dress up in. You're the champion, you are, kid. I reckon they ought to strike you a medal. You know what I'm telling you? You get sick, you get sicker than a dog and put yourself to bed, because if you turn up at cricket and pinch a game from another fellow you'll be the sorriest kid ever."

Josh bewildered, bewildered, moaning inside, fighting to stop it from showing. They were accusing him of things they were inventing. "It's not true. You kids couldn't pick the truth if you heard it. Why don't you ask Betsy about the cricket? Betsy, it wasn't like that, was it? It's the same with everything. Not like you say. I couldn't be that stupid. You must be talking about some other fellow."

Rex giggling and Betsy looking at the ground and Harry giving his pants a hitch. "Don't you turn up for cricket. You dig yourself a hole and crawl down it. If it wasn't for your auntie I'd flatten you now. I'd *flatten* you, Joshua."

Harry walking away like an ape, Rex going with him tossing pebbles between his hands, Betsy still standing in her pool of shadow, eyes downturned.

"Betsy." Josh saying it sadly.

Betsy glancing at him and drooping from the shoulders as if her head had become heavy, Josh suddenly wondering, but Harry was at the cemetery gate, waiting. "Come on, Betsy. What are you doing?"

"Betsy, I haven't told any tales, not about anything, I swear it." Wanting to go after her as she walked away, but afraid of Harry. "Betsy, I didn't tell Laura to jump off the bridge, I swear it. What really happened wasn't anything like it. Where do they get these stories? And I didn't threaten that little kid without a jolly good reason. He's a horror. Betsy why did you let Harry think those things about the cricket? Are you scared of him or something?"

But she had left him to it and he was talking to the trees.

Gosh, Josh, you're letting them wipe the floor with you. You'll have to go in with your fists swinging; it's the only thing they'll understand. All this nobleness and sweetness; they don't think that way. Dob 'em in, Josh; you can't be the martyr for ever. That Laura! Why protect her? What do you think you're proving? That there's a fool born every minute and every one is you?

Josh wandering back to Great-grandfather's grave to reread the inscription.

He always gave his fellow man the benefit of the doubt

"If it's true, Great-grandfather, you're a better man than I am."

A pebble bouncing on the gravestone with a tinkling sound, Rex grinning over the top of someone else's headstone. "You talking to a fairy?"

"Not you again …

"Who are you talking to?"

"Myself."

Rex leaning his elbows on the headstone. "You sweet on Betsy?"

"Go away or I'll clobber you."

"You won't clobber me."

"Don't be so sure."

"I'm sure. You sweet on Betsy?"

"What are you hanging round for?"

"I've been hangin' round all morning. I'm your shadow. It's good for a laugh. You're funnier than Laurel and Hardy. Do you want me to put in a word for you with Betsy?"

"No."

"Have you got a cigarette?"

"Have I got a *what*? Don't tell me you're another Sonny. I couldn't stand it."

"You mean Jimmy?"

"Yeh, I mean Jimmy."

"That's why you said you'd beat him up, isn't it?"

"Don't tell me you know it!"

"Yep."

"I suppose everyone knows it?"

"Mostly everyone."

"Well, why make out it was my fault?"

Rex shrugging. "Why not?"

"Because it's dishonest. Because it's not fair."

"He's only a little kid and he's pretty. We never beat him up. We just laugh at him. But you're a real droop. You don't laugh at anythin'. Do you want me to put in a word with Betsy?"

"No."

"She likes you."

"Yeh; like a toothache."

"She likes you. Honest injun. She's crazy."

"She's *told* you she likes me?"

"Nope. Betsy never tells anyone anythin'. Laura's a liar."

Josh sighing. "What are you trying to do? Stir up more trouble?"

"Not me."

"And I suppose everyone calls Laura a liar?"

"Not Harry." Rex flicking his pebbles one by one, sending them bouncing, tinkling, across gravestones.

"I wish you'd stop that! It's disrespectful."

"They don't mind. Lets 'em know we're still cooking. You want me to fix it for you with Betsy?"

"You couldn't fix anything, and I don't go round with girls, specially not with Harry's, even if she is your sister."

"She's not Harry's girl."

"You try telling that to Harry."

"Betsy's telling him all the time. But he's persistent. Laura's a slob."

"I don't know what you're up to, Rex, but I'm not falling for it. I'm not saying these things; you are."

"Don't you trust me?"

Josh going silent and suddenly anxious; Rex turning out to be more than a silly giggle.

"You've got to trust someone, haven't you? You're on the outer but I'm in the middle. Harry's like that. He's a good fella. Always fighting everyone's battles. Harry's a sucker. You ought to trust me. I'm your friend."

"You're my friend all right. You're setting me up for something.

And who started it? Who tripped me yesterday?"

Rex shrugging. "Not me."

"You *didn't* trip me?"

"Didn't say that. Said I didn't start it. You started it. You're a real droop. I reckon girls are crazy. I'll fix it for you with Betsy."

"I said *don't!*"

"You don't like Betsy?"

This kid's got more faces than a two-headed penny.

"Where you going?"

Josh walking away, not answering.

"Don't go to cricket. They'll get you."

Josh not doubting that for an instant, but walking away, saying nothing.

"If you go to cricket I won't get a game. I'm the wicket-keeper."

Josh swinging on his heel, shouting back at him, "Well, you won't be playing today!" Then striding home to Aunt Clara.

27

Sneaking down the passage with the empty shopping-basket, wondering how late it was, feeling downright irritable, spoiling for an argument. Floorboards creaking.

"Is that you, Josh?" Her voice coming sharply.

"Yes, Aunt Clara."

The kitchen door suddenly shutting, shutting him out, like curtain-fall on a half-finished performance. Aunt Clara's voice issuing from beyond it. "Put the shopping in the laundry. I'll sort it out later. And close the door in case the cat gets at it."

"Wouldn't it be handier in the kitchen?"

"No, it wouldn't."

The brush-off again!

Josh going through the motions of Aunt Clara's deception, picking things up and banging them down, slamming doors, maybe carrying it farther than Aunt Clara intended. Laura somewhere in the offing. That was obvious. Though there wasn't a sight of her.

"Josh."

"Yes, Aunt Clara."

"Dress for cricket, then come through for lunch. Bill brought your clothes over. They're waiting in the bedroom."

"It's not lunchtime, is it?"

"It will be. There's a good lad. Do as I ask you."

It will be! Yeh, and in a year it'll be Christmas. Heck, Aunt

Clara, there are things that have got to be put straight between us and now I'm shut out of the kitchen as if I had the measles. Blooming Laura! How long does it take her to do the scrubbing? You'd think she was scrubbing St Paul's Cathedral. Look, I'm not leaving this house again until we come to an understanding. Last night you knew everything but reckoned you knew nothing. Fighting off people coming here to flatten me and not even telling me. That's deceiving me, Aunt Clara. There I was trying to protect you and all the time you knew it. One thing on top of another. Shooting your mouth off about my poems. Forcing me into cricket; for your private information, Aunt Clara, I'm a dead-rotten player. Kicking me out of the house when I should have bally well stayed here and sorted it out with Laura. And what have my cousins been up to? I don't get it. Even if they are a bunch of so-and-so's how can it be my fault, how could it? I've behaved myself in this town like an angel because Dad threatened to kill me if I didn't. So saint-like I don't even know me. Maybe you're the trouble. Kids telling me you're mortgaged to the eyebrows. What a load of rubbish. Everyone in the family knows you could buy and sell the King of England. That's why Mum won't have a bar of you. Because of your blinking money. And then they say I'm sponging. Living on the smell of an oily rag! Have you ever heard such nonsense? House full of furniture. More furniture in the bathroom than we have in our living-room. What are they talking about? More books in the bedrooms than we've got in the public library. Carpets from Persia. Glass from Bohemia. Chelsea china. Strike me, she could start a museum. Sponging on her. What a lot of hogwash. Everyone in town must be a born liar. Living in the sun, you call it. It's like living down a drainpipe. What's wrong with my stupid cousins? They never told me Ryan Creek was a madhouse, and even Dad reckons it only wakes itself on Sundays for staggering off to church and staggering home again. By crikey, Great-grandfather, you've no idea what you started. A place like this is a national disaster. No wonder they stuck a slab of granite on you big enough to sink a warship. They had to put it there to stop you from leaping out again.

Someone ringing at the front doorbell shattering Josh's magnificent oration.

Bedroom door wide open. Josh half-naked in the middle of the carpet still wagging a finger at Great-grandfather's portrait. Footsteps coming up the passage. Josh making a snap decision to pull his pants on. Aunt Clara trotting past pretending not to notice, but stopping suddenly as if she'd met a barrier. "Good heavens, Josh, now I've seen everything." Then trotting on again. A remark, Aunt Clara, that I would not have expected from a lady. But feeling sort of peculiar as if he was waiting for some other fellow to climb in alongside him. Gathering up the waistband by the handful and shuffling to the mirror to check on the scenery. Standing there blinking as if he had never seen his own reflection. Then swearing. "The dirty dog. That lousy Bill. What's he done to me?"

Josh viewing himself from several angles, letting go the waistband and watching it drop to his ankles, pulling it up again and sighting his legs bare from the calves downwards. Pants made for a dwarf with a belly like an elephant. Josh, Josh, have you ever seen anything like it? If you hitch 'em up you'll need a periscope. If you drop 'em down you'll be indecent. Aunt Clara, they're trying to turn me into a monkey. Great-grandfather, don't you look at me or that slab of granite won't be heavy enough, you'll come shrieking up through the middle of it. Betsy, if you come to cricket I'll drop dead of mortification. I'll never catch the ball, I'll never bally well reach it, I'll have to run a yard before my pants start moving.

"Josh, may I come in without fear of embarrassment?"

"The door's open, Aunt Clara." A heart-rending voice of quiet desperation. "Everyone welcome. Be my guest."

"That's a strange thing to say, Josh, and a strange way to say it."

"It's a strange sight you're seeing, Aunt Clara. Whose clothes are they? I mean, what could wear them? It'd have to be an animal. A wombat maybe."

Aunt Clara taking off her spectacles and giving them a polish.

"All right," Josh adding. "Laugh your head off. It's got to start sometime. I might as well get used to it."

"They must be Freddie's. I'm surprised that Bill bothered to bring them."

"I'm not."

"He must have ridden out miles to get them."

"That figures."

Aunt Clara smiling. "We'll put a few pins in them, dear. Perhaps no one will notice."

"It'll need to be a very dark afternoon, Aunt Clara."

"You're a funny boy, Josh. You're really very funny."

"Thanks."

"I mean it as a compliment. You're quite an entertainment."

"Yeh."

"You are, dear. I judged you hastily. I'm going to miss you for more than your earnestness."

"I haven't gone yet, Aunt Clara."

"That was Rex at the door."

"Was it? If it had been Bill I'd have strangled him."

"The match is starting early. The boys from Croxley are here already. Rex thought you might not be able to make it. He wanted to know if your stomach-ache was worse."

"Haven't got a stomach-ache."

"He said you were sick in the cemetery."

"I wasn't."

"What were you doing in the cemetery?"

"Reading tombstones."

"And Rex. Was he reading them?"

"Rex and I had a difference of opinion." Why hide it any longer?

"Are you in trouble, Josh? Why don't you tell me? You're not getting on very well with people, are you?"

"You might say that, Aunt Clara."

"Whose fault is it?"

"Couldn't be theirs, could it? I mean, it would have to be mine, wouldn't it?"

"I didn't say that."

No, Josh, no, you're not to bring her into it. You don't cry for yourself, you cry for other people. She can't know everything. How could she? Button up the lip, Josh. "Please, Aunt Clara, have you got the pins handy? I can't hold these pants up much longer."

28

Aunt Clara calling, "Time's getting away, Josh."

There's a line, Aunt Clara, between two kinds of laughter and these kids don't know the difference. I'm sick of being on the wrong end of it and I'm not feeling too good. I feel terrible, honest. Walking out of this house pinned up like a baby in a napkin. It's not fair, Aunt Clara, I can't do it. I can't walk down the passage even to the kitchen. Expecting me to face a giggling Laura. Taking it from her, I reckon, will be harder than taking it from anybody. And those kids say they're going to get me.

"Josh, you'd better hurry."

Suddenly shouting back at her. "I can't."

"Yes, you can. I know you're ready."

Something firm about it, overruling him, not allowing for argument. The old Plowman way of never listening. Telling him. Like Dad in a huff. Like all the uncles and cousins and the aunts who were Plowmans before they got married. Where do they get it from, Great-grandfather? Or did you have it, too, and she's covering up the evidence?

"Come along, Josh."

It's like a chain round your neck, pulling you. No matter how hard you pull back you can't break it. You've got to do as they say, always, and if you don't they can't understand you and turn nasty. Coming to the curtains, rustling and chafing. You'll remember these curtains until the day they bury you. They symbolize something. A threshold of disaster.

Kitchen door ajar, knocking at it, all tensed up because of Laura. Aunt Clara sounding surprised or amused or something. "Why are you knocking?"

"Because I thought I had to. I've been getting shut out of it so often."

"Josh, don't exaggerate. Laura's gone, if that's what's troubling you. Ten minutes ago out the back way."

Feeling sick from relief and reaching out to the wall and sagging melodramatically against it.

"Your lunch is cut. I'll have it wrapped in a jiffy."

Getting his breath back only for a moment. Suddenly losing it again. "Haven't I the time to eat it?" Thinking of carrots and lettuce leaves and hunks of wholemeal like door-stops exposed to public ridicule.

"Not a chance. You only have a couple of minutes. You mustn't keep Bill waiting."

Moping into the kitchen as if walking on eggshells, wondering how soon the pins were going to start popping open and feeling more and more frightened, longing for sympathy, the cry on the inside breaking through to the surface. "Aunt Clara. ..."

Watching her freeze in the act of bunching up carrots. "Yes, Josh, what is it?"

"Do I look too awful? I can only take so much, Aunt Clara."

Offering a hand to him for comfort, but Josh suddenly regretting his weakness, suddenly remembering all his self-imposed promises. Shaking his head again, clenching his fists again, stepping away from her.

"Are they making your life difficult?"

Looking at the floor. "I don't want to tell tales. ..."

"I know you don't and I respect you for it. But we're family, aren't we?"

Nodding at the floor.

"That's what families are for, lightening the load a little, but I can't help if you won't let me."

Trying to harden himself, but it was a terrible struggle. "According to the kids you've been doing a lot of helping already."

"And you'd rather I didn't?"

"I don't know, Aunt Clara, but I wish you'd level with me." Feeling the bits falling apart again. "I don't know whether I'm coming or going. There seem to be too many things against me. I can't win at anything."

"You want to *win* something, Josh?"

"You know I don't mean that." Almost pleading. "Don't make it sound all different. It's just that everything I do goes haywire."

"Well, I did say, didn't I, that you take things rather seriously. I think you take them too seriously."

"But I don't." Beating around trying to find the words he wanted. "Honest, I'm trying to see the funny side all the time. I always do, Aunt Clara, whether you believe it or not."

"You say some funny things, Josh, but that's not quite the same."

"I don't know what you mean. ..."

"I think you do. Comedy can be a very serious business for you, and for other people like you; that doesn't mean you're light-hearted. When I talk about sunshine, Josh, it's sunshine that I mean. Laughing on the outside, but crying on the inside; I don't mean that at all."

"I'm not with you, Aunt Clara. You're way over my head." A pit of melancholy. "And it's letting you down that's my worry. Always letting you down but trying so hard not to. And look at me now. Like a scarecrow. They'll kill themselves laughing. Why have they got it in for me?"

"That was cruel of Bill, and it must have been deliberate. He's disappointed me."

"But I don't want you to be disappointed in him, Aunt Clara. I don't want you to be disappointed in anybody. I suppose it's got to be my fault somewhere. They're so nice to you. They do all sorts of things for you. I mean, they *live* here with you and I've only been around since Saturday. They scrub your house and chop your wood and clean your windows and dig your garden. They do all these things for nothing, just because they like you. They're better than I am, Aunt Clara. I do things for people, too, but because they pay me."

"Perhaps the situation is different, Josh. It's not wrong to expect payment."

"But they told me you're poor and that I'm sponging on you." Pleading now, well and truly, not able to get his voice down to a proper level. "You're not poor, Aunt Clara, are you?"

Aunt Clara somehow not responding, somehow looking as if she hadn't heard, although obviously she had. "Did they say that?"

"You couldn't be poor. I don't know how much things cost, Aunt Clara, but the things you've got in this house must be worth a fortune."

Aunt Clara still with a blank look about her, as if not understanding. "That's exactly what they are worth, Josh, a fortune."

"Well, why did they say it?"

"That's the question, Josh. Why did they say it?"

The doorbell. How long had it been ringing? Aunt Clara stirring herself, thrusting packets in a paper-bag with odd intensity. "You'd better go, I think." Pushing his lunch at him. "Don't keep Bill waiting."

"Aunt Clara, I don't want to go any more. I just can't go any more. People are going to see me. They're going to laugh at me. I look terrible. I'll shame you."

Something hard growing into Aunt Clara that made her look like other Plowmans. "You'll never shame me. You go out and show them what you're made of. I don't think they know. And I'll not come to spoil it or embarrass you. You go out and do it on your own."

Josh feeling as if he wanted to lie down and cry. "I'm not much of a cricketer, honest I'm not. I couldn't keep wickets to save my life, honest I couldn't. I don't want to go. I'm only taking Rex's game away from him."

Aunt Clara holding wide the kitchen door. "You're not going to disappoint me, Josh, are you?"

"Please, Aunt Clara."

She was looking harder and harder. "Or is there some other reason why you're trying to get out of it?"

The doorbell was sharp with impatience and Josh was hunting frantically for justification. "You're not consistent, Aunt Clara."

"Aren't I?"

"You kept me away from Laura. You pushed me out of the house. You as good as told me she didn't matter."

"Did you want to see Laura?"

"No, I didn't, but that's not the point. You pushed me then and you're pushing me again. I should have seen Laura. I should have faced her."

"All right. That was my mistake. I'm sorry. But whose mistake is it if you allow Bill to go without you?"

Oh, you're a cute one, Aunt Clara. Oh, that's playing dirty. ...

"Come on, pull yourself together. You're a Plowman."

Meeting her in the eye with sudden and open hostility and slapping his lunch on the table. "I can't eat that stuff in front of other people. Why don't you give me an honest sandwich!"

Crashing through the curtains and running to the front door.

29

Bill up at street level looking daggers. "So you're coming?"

Josh glaring back at him and slamming the door behind him, rattling the stained-glass panels.

"Yeh."

Thudding up the steps two at a time propelled by anger, leaping the last three to the top landing, counting a total of seven.

"Yeh, I'm coming."

Grabbing the gate from Bill's hand, rudely jolting him, and slamming that also, wrenching the spring from its socket, leaving it hanging.

"Yeh, I'm coming, O'Connor. Do you want to make something of it?" Full of recklessness, full of daring, sighting Rex on the opposite footpath and maybe a dozen boys waiting. "I'm ripe for you, O'Connor, and if there's any getting to be done I'll be doing it."

Bill gaping.

Josh leaping the ditch to the road, challenging the pins to start popping. Not caring. His pants could have dropped to his ankles. He'd have kicked them into the gutter and marched on in his underwear. Not caring.

Bill looking bewildered, coming behind, lagging.

"Have a laugh, you kids, get it over. Me and my twin brother. We're all in these pants together. Bill's idea of what's fitting and proper. Go on, O'Connor, laugh your head off and I'll rip your own off you."

Bill grabbing for his trousers instinctively, holding the waist-band, as startled as if something harmless and familiar had suddenly turned lethal.

"I've had you, O'Connor, by the bucketful. She knows now. She's heard it. You've pushed me into it. You had to make it happen. So now you can get me for a jolly good reason. Now you can try, O'Connor, but I'll be ready. Where's the cricket ground?"

Josh in the middle of the road proclaiming, standing to attention, not aware of it. "Come on, where's the cricket ground? I thought you were all steamed up with impatience."

"Hey, ease up, mate." Bill crimson with embarrassment, nervously rubbing his wrist against the hip of his trousers, perhaps trying not to notice people or praying that his mother was out of earshot. "Hey, you'll blow a valve or something. *I'm* the captain."

"Where's the cricket ground? Let's get on with it. Let's pulverize these kids from Croxley. That's what you're going to do with them, isn't it?"

Bill getting rattled. "Hey, will you stop your shouting. What are you trying to do to us? Start a riot?"

"Come on, O'Connor, let's get stuck into them, or aren't you playing?"

"Strike me, stop your shouting! Are you off your rocker?" Bill not knowing where to put himself, losing track of what he was saying. "You're the one that won't be playing. I'm the captain. You take orders from me or get a thumping."

"Talking about blood-noses, O'Connor?"

"That's what I'm talking about, Plowman."

"Right you are. Do you want yours now? Here? In the middle of the road?"

Bill not coping as well as he wanted to, getting hotter and hotter,

Josh still shouting at him. "You can push me so far, O'Connor, and no farther. Will you have yours now? Here?"

Bill screeching. "You don't reckon on giving *me* a blood-nose, you skinny streak of misery! I'll spread you all over the gutter."

Josh sticking his jaw out. "Go ahead. Try it." Words coming he had no control over. Bill standing totally disconcerted, his own front fence ahead of him, Miss Clara Plowman's behind him, but so far committed there was no backing out of it.

"Come on, O'Connor, you've been telling me you'd get me. Here's your opportunity. Dead easy. All your mates to help you."

Josh shaping up like a boxer, Bill coming looking ghastly, kids in white clothes spilling from the footpaths yelling, Rex darting in looking frantic, "No, Bill, no, you mustn't." Gates swinging, a motor-horn blowing, cycle bells ringing, someone shouting, "Off the road, you kids. You're holding up the traffic."

Bill growing bigger and bigger—an alarming illusion of Josh's last-moment panic—but then recklessly rushing, pummelling furiously and knowing instantly he wasn't hurting him. Bill was hard and Josh had thought he would be softer. Hitting him was hurting the wrong person and every blow that Bill threw back came like a hammer, Josh unable to block them. Bill wading in forcing Josh from the road to the gutter, stumbling on the gutter, falling backwards. Bill standing over him, his face twisted, rubbing one fist into the palm of the other.

"Get up, Plowman."

Kids standing back for safety, legs and faces, one face like Betsy as stark as a black-and-white picture, another vaguely like Aunt Clara as if she was crying, all seen in a moment.

Josh scrambling up with a pain in his ribs and a noise in his head like a locomotive, stumbling inexplicably, kids shrilling with laughter, and a driving thud against his shoulder that sent him spinning.

"Get up, Plowman."

But he couldn't. Pins were sticking into him, his breath was hurting and his trousers were at his knees and he couldn't drag them up again. He was lying in the gutter where Bill had said he would put him.

Closing his eyes on it, not wanting to see, or hear, or know; humiliated. Over in seconds, finished in seconds, flattened.

Hands under his armpits; too shattered to resist them; lifting him to his feet. Expecting another punch, flinching from it, expecting more, but someone was dragging his trousers up and talking with the voice of a man. "Are you all right, boy?"

Josh sagging in the man's arms, nodding, though whether he was hurt or not hurt he didn't know for certain. Struggling to stand on his own but wanting, really, to sink again. Trying to hold his trousers, wondering whether his eyes were blackened or his nose bled or his ribs were broken, wondering whether he could ever hold up his head and cross the street again. It's no good, Aunt Clara; doing things physically is not my way.

"Bill." The voice of the man. "It wasn't an even match. You're older and forty pounds heavier."

"I didn't start it, Mr. Cotton."

"I know you were provoked. Everyone in the street heard that. But it was an uneven match. Nothing to be proud of, Bill. No excuse for taking it past the first punch. You, young Plowman, can only blame yourself. Don't you know to pick fights your own weight?"

Josh looking at the ground, trying to hold his head up but it wouldn't come, not knowing who the man was, though the name was in his mind somewhere. Trying to recognize people from their feet, Aunt Clara's not there! He could have sworn he had seen her face.

"Why did you start it? People laughing at your trousers? You'd do better to laugh back at them." Not an unkind voice but a firm one, accustomed to authority.

Josh saying nothing, trying to lift his head, trying to find Betsy's feet, trying to pluck out the pin that was pricking at his hip. Trying, trying to pull himself together, sick to death of disgrace.

"You're not crying are you, boy?"

"No." Defiantly.

"Well, lift yourself up."

Josh suddenly remembered *Cotton*, the schoolmaster who wouldn't give Laura her marks, and brought his head up suddenly, expecting to meet an ogre, wanting to dislike him, ready to hate him. A gentle-looking man, probably sixty, grey-haired and stooped a little. Dressed in white with a black silk coat and floppy hat, and pale-brown eyes that met him squarely. Nothing there to hate even though he had not given Laura her marks when she was eleven. The man taking Josh by the chin and looking him over. "A few bruises. Nothing to worry about. You're tougher than you look."

"I can take a beating, sir, if I have to."

"Where'd you get the scratch from?"

"Yesterday, from falling over."

"Fighting?"

"No, sir. I don't make a habit of it."

"I thought you did, the way you provoked this one. Extraordinary. You mustn't blame Bill for it. You'll have to apologize."

Aunt Clara not there, Betsy not there, only grown-ups and strangers and Bill and his mother. Bill not very happy, his mother looking anguished as if her son had been caught destroying sacred property. Whispering fiercely at him, holding him by the elbow, her lips forming the magic word *Plowman*. Josh suddenly sick of it, sick of everything, and waddling off across the road holding his pants up, suffering the pinpricks, his ribs still hurting. Footsteps behind him and a hand on his shoulder. "Where are you off to?"

Josh trying to shake himself free, but that gentle man had a large hand and a strong one. "To my aunt's, Mr. Cotton. There's nowhere else that I know of."

"You wish to upset her?"

"I don't wish to upset anyone, but it seems I can't help it. Will you let me go, sir."

Mrs. O'Connor was in front of him also. "Don't go, Josh. What about your cricket?"

"What about it?"

"*You've got to play.*"

"I can't play cricket, Mrs.O'Connor. I don't *want* to."

"You're going to let them beat you?"

"I don't know what you mean."

"Of course you know, Josh. Provoked, you say, Mr. Cotton? This is the boy who was provoked, I'm ashamed to tell you. Treated like this and he's a Plowman."

Josh wrenching his shoulder free with tight lips and determination and leaving them to argue, opening the gate, fifteen steps down, descending to the doorway.

Aunt Clara waiting. Yes, she had seen him; she was still crying.

"That wasn't what I meant, Josh. That wasn't the way to do it."

"How would you have done it with your pants down round your ankles?"

"Oh, Josh. ..."

"It's done, Aunt Clara. There's no going back on it."

She took him in and shut the door behind them.

30

Josh perched on the side of the ridiculous bed half-expecting the tinkling chandelier to come crashing round his ears. Why shouldn't it? Everything else had happened. Then they'd cart him up to the cemetery and all have a party and chip the words in his headstone:

Here lies Josh Plowman
Failure
He tried to give them the benefit of the doubt
and look where it got him

Trousers kicked into a heap of dishonour in the centre of the carpet (kicked there and jumped upon several times), locked in with Great-grandfather in all his regalia but conducting no conversations with him. There was nothing he could say to Great-grandfather; his expression was not sympathetic. It is not, Josh, strictly speaking, the kind of problem that one can discuss with an ancestor.

Perched on the bed-edge, balancing, numbed bodily as if he had been run over, rubbing his scratches and caressing his bruises and dying slowly from humiliation. Go home, Josh. Pack your bag and get out of it. Mum was right in the first place. Hitch a ride, walk, crawl on your hands and knees, but for Pete's sake get started even if there isn't another train until tomorrow.

Knockings at the front door like knockings upon a sepulchre, as if ringing the bell was much too frivolous. Trouble coming, Josh. Dressing hurriedly, thinking of hiding under the bed or in the wardrobe or departing through the window.

Voices of conspiracy murmuring, moving down the passage, stopping at his door, man voices and woman voices. Sounding like a multitude. Deputation from the workers.

"Josh. Mr. Cotton wants a word with you."

"I've got nothing to say to Mr. Cotton or to anyone."

Aunt Clara sounding like a Plowman. "Unlock your door. Shutting yourself in solves nothing."

"There's nothing to solve."

"We cannot agree with you. Open the door."

Turning the key reluctantly, like stepping in front of a gun timed to go off at irregular intervals. "It's open. ..."

"That won't do. You're to come into the passage."

"Gosh, Aunt Clara, hasn't there been enough trouble!"

"Trouble a-plenty, but let's see if we can settle it."

Opening the door slowly, expecting a passage full of people. Only two of them. Josh instantly vowing to be calm and totally stubborn. Swearing off allegiance to everybody except Josh Plowman. Giving Aunt Clara the cold eye reserved for the most acute moments of family disagreement.

"Mr. Cotton and a gentleman from Croxley are the umpires. They've been talking things over. They will accept you on the field neatly dressed in any way that pleases you."

Somehow he had seen that coming. "I'm not playing."

"If you don't, Josh, Bill won't be able to play either."

"That's Bill's bad luck. He should have thought of it earlier."

The schoolmaster said, "Mrs. O'Connor is adamant and so is everyone concerned. Until you shake hands, the pair of you, there won't be any cricket."

Josh twitching his nose although endeavouring not to. "That's unfair to other people."

"Very."

"But not my fault. Nothing to do with me."

"*Everything* to do with you, boy."

"Nothing to do with me. It's petty. Classroom logic. I thought school was on holidays."

"Josh!" Aunt Clara flaring. "That's unforgivable. You will not be rude."

"Nothing rude about it, Aunt Clara. It's true. Would you turn me into a liar?"

The schoolmaster coughing. "Allow me, Miss Plowman. This boy is no fool. We're not imposing classroom logic as you call it. Don't mistake me. I suppose it could be called petty from one viewpoint or loyalty from another. It hasn't come from the umpires. It has come from the players. The agreement is that if you will not take the field and Bill cannot take the field neither will any of the others and Croxley will have to go home disappointed. In my school, for your information, young Plowman, there would be no such condition. I'd drop the pair of you and start the game without you."

"It's blackmail."

"That's an odd word, boy."

"They're pushing it all onto me. It's got nothing to do with shaking hands. I know what's behind it. They're asking me to accept the blame for everything, and when they get me out there they'll not be bowling at the wickets, they'll be bowling at yours truly."

"Josh!" Aunt Clara exclaiming. "That's a dreadful thing to say."

"It's true."

"A most unlikely happening, boy. The umpires wouldn't stand for it."

"The umpires wouldn't have much say in it."

"No, no, boy. You don't win cricket matches by bowling at the wicket-keeper. Has someone threatened you?"

"I'm not telling tales, Mr. Cotton, but I wouldn't play cricket with your kids if it was the last game on earth. Tell them no. Tell them find another sucker."

"Josh!"

"That's the way it is, Aunt Clara."

"You're a bad loser!"

"It has nothing to do with losing, Aunt Clara."

"But it might have something to do with fairness, would you say that, boy?"

"I would, Mr. Cotton. That's just what I'd say."

The schoolmaster shaking his head. "I think you mistake me. I mean *your* sense of fairness to others. A little bit of forgive and forget. They're not undesirables, these boys. I don't like to hear them spoken of in this manner. It's a big day in their lives. The cricket match has happened every year for half a century, and it lies with you to make it or wreck it."

"You're always strictly fair yourself, Mr. Cotton?"

The schoolmaster's eyes glinting. "Is that a question?"

"I meant it to be."

"I was not under the impression I was here to be interrogated, but I try to be fair. I believe I have that reputation, though I would not expect you to have heard of it."

"You couldn't make a mistake?"

"You mean now?"

"I mean any time."

"Josh, Josh!"

"Leave him to me, Miss Plowman. I'm used to young fellows stretching their wings. Yes, of course I can make a mistake, boy. Can't you?"

"Yes, sir, but it's one of your mistakes I'm thinking of."

There was nothing gentle in the schoolmaster's eyes any longer. "I think you had better explain yourself."

"When Laura Jones was eleven she wrote a poem. It was worth eight out of ten, coming from her. Why didn't you give it to her? You've no idea, Mr. Cotton, what you've done to Laura."

"Laura Jones wrote a poem, did she? Worth eight out of ten? When she was eleven? She could have, I suppose, but I have no particular memory of it. Should I? How many marks did I give her, if you're so well informed?"

"None. You accused her of copying it. You told her she cheated. And the class laughed."

Aunt Clara almost shouting. "You are under no obligation to answer, Mr. Cotton. I apologize. I am profoundly sorry that you should be insulted under my roof. I don't know what's come over him."

"I'll answer him. He has the style of a formidable adversary roused upon a matter of conscience. I am not insulted, Miss Plowman, but I am curious. As it so happens, I do recall the incident and she did copy the poem, of course."

"From what, sir?"

"I have no idea. But from any of a hundred publications contributed to by children that she might have read."

"Read and remembered and written down afterwards during a class exercise?"

"Oh yes, boy. For a specific purpose, yes."

"And still known, every word of it, years later?"

"That's interesting, if it's the case, but I see no reason to change my mind."

"It was a simple poem, Mr. Cotton, not a clever one. I know she wrote it."

"Do you? I wish I could share your certainty, but perhaps you still have a little to learn about human nature. It can be a disappointing phenomenon, wouldn't you agree, Miss Plowman?"

If you nod to that, Aunt Clara, after all you've told me about believing in people. ...

Aunt Clara sighing, Aunt Clara nodding, and Josh going colder and colder. "I'm not changing my mind either, no sir. I'm not playing cricket. I'm not carrying the can for them. Let's see *them* stick to a principle for a change." Deliberately stepping back into his room and quickly turning the key.

"Josh!"

Not answering. Not any more. Our worlds are not the same, Aunt Clara. If you're sticking to yours, I'm sticking to mine.

"Josh, you can't do this."

I've done it, Aunt Clara. It's done.

Rappings at the door. "If this is to be your attitude, I think you'd better start packing. You can go on the morning train."

That suits me, Aunt Clara. That suits me down to the ground.

Murmurings going away.

31

So it ends in anger and disgrace and distress and everything else you'd care to put your tongue around. You name it, Josh, and it ends that way. You're the daddy of all the Plowmans, that's what they tell you, and maybe they're right. You've ripped through Ryan Creek like a runaway truck. Every kid in town hates your guts.

Every kid outside in the street. Every kid waiting at the cricket ground. Every kid asking himself what sort of a louse is Josh.

Everyone up there at the gate; Aunt Clara apologizing, apologizing, apologizing to everyone in sight.

No one told me the match was so important. I thought it was a kid's game. Grown-up umpires. People coming to watch. I couldn't have played anyway. It's out of my class. What's wrong with Aunt Clara? Push, push, push. I didn't tell her I was a champion. I only told her I played. Wasn't that good enough?

Home to Mum. That's next. She'll ask what's the trouble—you're not expected back till Saturday or Sunday or maybe Monday?

The trouble, Mum, they tell me, is that I'm a louse. But I'm a fair enough kid, aren't I? I don't go stirring up trouble. I don't hate people. The neighbours don't lock up their houses when they see me coming. I haven't an enemy in the world that I can think of right now. But from the minute I hit the place everything went wrong. They had it in for me like I was poison; even Aunt Clara turned nasty when things wouldn't go the way she wanted. And that I'll never understand. She took their side, not mine, and they were wrong all along the line. They never even tried to be right.

Josh, you didn't behave like a Plowman, did you?

I behaved like me.

You must be a Plowman, Josh. You must wear it all over you not knowing it's there. A Plowman doesn't need to be wrong. He can be objectionable when he's right.

Mum, should I have played? Should I go even now? All these kids waiting for their game. Kids coming from Croxley, miles and miles. Betsy hating me. But you don't know about her. There's something about Betsy that strikes a little bell. I'd go if she asked me; I reckon I'd run all the way. You can't always put a principle first, can you, Mum? Sometimes you've got to compromise. It looks that way if Aunt Clara's any guide. She's turning herself inside-out so often I don't know which face is properly hers. Honest, Mum, it's a laugh. Everyone threatening they'd get me if I went to the match, then holding me up to ransom when I decided not to play.

If I wasn't a Plowman none of this would have happened to me. If stupid Bill hadn't brought those pants it wouldn't have happened. If Laura hadn't jumped from the bridge, if Rex hadn't tripped me, if Aunt Clara hadn't taken my book of poems, if I hadn't come away from you and Dad, if a hundred things hadn't happened it wouldn't have happened at all. I ask you. It's a horrible rolling wheel. What hope has a fellow got? The day he gets born it starts turning and he can't even jump out of the way. What's wrong with people? Have they always got to find a mug they can blame?

32

Was Aunt Clara in the house or hadn't she returned? Time was the problem, not knowing it, trying to estimate its passage. Two o'clock; three o'clock; heaven knew what it was. Clocks everywhere, in the dining-room and parlour and in every room but this, and not one striking. The whole house silent except for tinklings and rustlings. The street silent as if the town lay sleeping, as if every child had gone to his cot and every dog to his mat and every adult to his hammock in the sun. Cows chewing the cud, not lowing. Birds in the shade, not singing. Wind intermittently dying as if weary of blowing. Josh on his bed all clothes packed except those he was wearing, wondering whether he should unlock the door and quietly go exploring, tired of being hungry, tired of being restless, tired of impatience.

No train until the morning. The morning comes tomorrow. Tomorrow is an eternity too far off to think about. Don't wait, Josh, start walking.

Walking home to Melbourne would be an adventure, better than train travel and Aunt Clara has your ticket anyway. Dragging your bag, that'd be murder, but escaping from this place would be worth almost anything.

Walking home to Melbourne, sleeping under haystacks, drinking from the rivers, eating from the orchards. Leave the bag behind, Josh, bundle up your woollens, put your poems in your pocket and get yourself going.

Why be frightened? Who's going to hurt you? Singing in the sunshine. Counting stars at night-time. Making up poems. No one to worry you. There's adventure for you. A boy and a continent getting to know each other, travelling the roads that history made before you, pushing through the bush like Great-grandfather. Gosh, Josh, if only you could do it. Could you make it real? Could you lift it from the story-books and live it? Talk about romantic. Simply terrific.

Josh, start walking. A hundred miles to Melbourne. Home by Saturday or Sunday or maybe Monday. School doesn't start until next Wednesday. What about it, Josh? What do you reckon?

Would they come looking for you—police and rescue parties and hairy-legged bush-walkers? Would it be written up in all the newspapers and get properly spoilt? Or would they recognize that other kids, even younger, were out in the world earning a living, coping with the rough and tumble?

Writing on a page carefully removed from the middle of his poetry book. Shaking all over.

Dear Aunt Clara,

I'm sorry I have disappointed you and I don't want you to fall out with your friends because of me, but I'd like to finish my holiday. It's the first holiday I've had since we went to Dromana and lived in a shack. Will you please put my bag on the train and send it home to Mum. I think walking will be much more fun than being sent home in disgrace. I'm fourteen and a half and quite able to look after myself and I don't want people searching for me making fuss because I'm not lost and I'm not running away. All I'm doing is walking home. Please send Mum a telegram. I expect to be there by Monday at the latest. Love, Josh.

Choosing from his bag a few extra clothes and his spare pair of shoes and rolling them neatly inside his raincoat. A bundle like a sheaf of hay with the belt drawn tightly, a loop hanging free to carry it by. Trying it over his shoulder, then remembering he had no money.

Should he go the long way and really look for it, where Sonny fished for yabbies, where Harry killed the rabbit, where Laura had him running? Carefully over that ground once again, then on into the yellow distance beyond the bridge whether or not he had found it, along the road through the stubble chewing wheat and picking blackberries and keeping a weather eye open for anything edible. The road had to go to Melbourne; the finger-post said so. Take the long road, Josh, and that'll trick them. Who would expect it?

What do you reckon, Great-grandfather? It's not the coward's way—is it?—turning loss into profit. You know the old parable about the talents. If you've got 'em use 'em. If you're chucked out on your ear make the best of it. I'm disappointed in Aunt Clara, Great-grandfather, and she is your daughter. I'm not going into details, but she's sure not perfect and that's my considered opinion. I would have thought that by the time you got to seventy-three you'd have all the answers, but she's performing like an amateur. Can't pick right from wrong. Imagine it, Great-grandfather, taking their side as if I was nothing to her. Nagging me to tell her what it was all about, then turning against me as soon as I told her. Believing them, not me, and they're nothing but a bunch of liars. Except Betsy. But that's over, isn't it? Before it even started. At least you had Rosemary Caroline Plowman (*née Braddock*) long enough to get to know her.

Adding a note to the foot of Aunt Clara's letter.

PS. I don't know what Great-grandfather would say about this, getting to your age and not being able to pick right from wrong. Love, J.

 PPS. Send Betsy to an elocution teacher so she can learn to speak properly. She sounds like the lady [Please Turn Over] in our fish shop. And I'm not being a snob.

Folding it carefully, with reverence. After all, it was important. Writing *Aunt Clara* on the outside and placing it prominently on his pillow, trembling violently, almost sick with nerves. Standing back to look at it from several angles, then slinging his roll and moving quietly to the door.

Pause a moment, Josh.

Are you sure?

It's not impulse, Mum, honest. There's nothing hasty about it. I know I might go hungry. I know I'll get horribly wet and horribly hot and horribly dirty. I know that sleeping under the stars mightn't be all it's cracked up to be. I know it's a long way and my feet are going to get sore. I know I'll arrive home looking like the wreck of the Hesperus. But it's making something good out of a bad job. That's what it's doing, Mum.

Turning the key. Edging open the door. Three distinct groans on the hinges, each groan like a cow in pain. Having to breathe with his mouth open. Sweat trickling from his armpits. Knees so weak they were all but knocking together.

The passage empty. The front door open. Hot breezes rolling along the passage and dancing through the curtains. The crystal leaves behind him tinkling like an alarm bell. Almost panicking. Hastily pulling on the bedroom door to muffle the noises, lock clicking loudly. All sounds positively explosive.

Panting.

Next crisis, Josh. What if she sees you? What if she tries to stop you? Do you push past her, do you break out, do you run?

Trying to silence the thunder in his head, trying to listen. There could have been twenty people milling in the house and he'd have been none the wiser. Pressing a hand to his brow, wondering whether the strain was worth it.

It's more than trotting to the door, Josh, and heading off into the wide blue yonder. I mean, how do you walk the length of the house, down through the middle of it, completely undetected? Creaky old floorboards down there, squeaky old spring on the screen door, fat white George to shoot out his sharp claws, Aunt Clara outside maybe, in a cane chair in the shade getting rained on by rose petals, cat-napping as light as a feather.

It's got to be the front way, Josh. Creep out the front and creep round the side and *lift your feet*. For once in your life see if you can cover a hundred yards without falling over.

Treading lightly to the front door, peering out through the screen, Scanning the picket fence up there from end to end or as much of it as he could see. Suddenly swearing in despair. Someone's head and shoulders up there, someone dressed in white, restlessly leaning on the fence as if he had been keeping watch for hours.

Stepping back hastily into the gloom, his heart hammering.

Gosh, Josh. Some rotten kid waiting for you in his cricket clothes. They couldn't have played their game after all. They must have stuck to their word. Would you believe it? And if they're waiting in front they'll be waiting at the back. They'll be waiting all around. What's wrong with Aunt Clara? Doesn't she care? How could anyone stand up there and Aunt Clara not know? You can't break out through a wall of kids. Only one of you and mobs of them. Holy cow, it's like trying to get out of prison.

Look, you've made up your mind. You're going and that's all there is to it. She's not marching you down to the station in the morning to *expel* you! Not on your life, she's not doing that to you.

It's got to be the back way, Josh, and if Aunt Clara's there you'll have to bust out past her and run like crazy. Let 'em catch you if they can. That's one thing you can do when you've got to. You can run like crazy.

Lock the bedroom door, why don't you? Put the key in your pocket! Be a little bit sneaky. She mightn't hear you; she mightn't stop you. I mean, you *could* get outside, couldn't you? And if the kids are waiting at the bottom fence they haven't got to see you. You can go to earth, can't you? You can hide in the garden until later, until dark if needs be. You're a step ahead, Josh; don't lose it. And won't Aunt Clara suppose you're still in your room? Being sulky. Being stubborn. Not answering. By the time she wakes up to it you'll be singing to the moon.

Doing it, by crikey. Quietly recovering the key from the inside, quietly locking it on the outside, quietly heading along the passage towards the back of the house, floorboards groaning, curtains rustling, it was a living wonder his shoes weren't squeaking. Passing every door in a sweat and a tremble. Sighting a clock, reading two-fifty. Locked in that room for three solid hours! But getting a feeling of emptiness around him, a growing certainty that Aunt Clara wasn't near him. Peeping into the kitchen. His lunch-bag still on the table where he had slapped it down in anger. Nothing touched from the moment he had stalked out to the High Street before noon. Nothing eaten. Nothing tidied away. Aunt Clara not anywhere to be seen.

Clear, Josh! You're in the clear!

Relaxing as if every sinew had suddenly stretched. A wild elation. You'll do it, Josh, you'll do it. Two steps in front. Two steps now.

Snatching up his lunch, gathering apples and unwashed carrots and the block of cheese, enough for a couple of extra meals, enough for one pocket stuffed full. Don't worry; it gives nothing away; she knows you've got to eat. She'll reckon you've eaten it in your room.

Josh, Josh, you're going to do it.

Darting to the back door. Aunt Clara not out there either. Not in her cane chair. Nowhere visible in the garden. Is it going too well? Who cares. Pushing the door open only far enough to squeeze out sideways, even fat white George not there to wave a claw at him. Gosh, Josh, has your luck turned? It's about time. It's the law of averages. Sooner or later it's got to bend your way.

Pressing against the wall among the stag ferns and fuchsias and masses of cat mint spilling from baskets. Talk about Moses in the bulrushes. Peering out through the foliage, weighing up his chances of getting to the fence-line against chances of being sighted. Too many places for kids to lie in, too many corners for them to hide around, too much open ground to cover after he got there. Step under the wire and they could mow him down from a dozen directions. Yeh, be sneaky, Josh. Be real sneaky. Go to earth and wait for later.

33

"George! Where are you?"

Aunt Clara calling, sounding irritable.

Josh dropping flat in the dirt in abject astonishment. God-fathers! She couldn't have been ten yards behind him.

Screen door squawking like a fowl being throttled. Tin plate getting slapped down on the bluestone. Josh lying as flat as a lizard shaking with heartbeats, praying for Aunt Clara to be stricken with a moment of blindness.

"George! Your liver."

Fronds of asparagus round about him, a man-sized patch of them, full-blown and feathery turning the sky luminous, green veins and green shadows and sunlight glitter, all in shivering motion. As a field-mouse might glance up to view the universe. Practically transparent, and only thirty feet from the veranda!

Going too well? His life-story in a nutshell. With her hand to the gate, no doubt, as he squeezed out the back way. With her nose in the door before he started down the garden. So close it wasn't funny.

Josh lying motionless trying to be a chameleon.

Aunt Clara in and out of the squawking screen door three times in as many minutes. Aunt Clara tossing tea-leaves far and wide from the veranda, Josh in panic feeling the sprinkles. Why couldn't she put her feet up and rest like an old woman? Aunt

Clara bustling down the path to the Throne Room and bustling back again talking to herself as if she had an audience. Calling herself Clara. All the Plowmans must be crackers. Talking to the teapot and talking to the box of kindling wood. Talking to the breeze littering up her bluestone with rose petals. "George, if you don't come for your liver, the flies will take it."

Mighty flies. Massed in formation. Roaring off with half a bullock!

"Why won't that boy answer? He's a second Maximilian. Heaven preserve me from pig-headed males who want to die for their principles as if in ten minutes it's still going to matter. Too perfect to live with. Oh, Clara, what a life he's got ahead of him. Who'll ever put up with him? His poor, poor mother. No wonder she's kept him on a chain like a prize poodle. George!" Shrilling. "Will you come home for your liver, you fat Casanova. If you're chasing she-cats, I'll lock you in the laundry."

Josh blushing. Aunt Clara, your language.

Aunt Clara gone, door squawking behind her. Gone, but for how many seconds? She's like a bee in a bottle. Gosh, Josh. Is this how spinster ladies carry on when there's no one to listen? And is *that* what she thinks of you *and* of Great-grandfather? The horrible old woman.

Wriggling farther down the garden as fast as he could wriggle. Slap into the raspberry patch. Like a jungle. Raspberries down his neck and spider webs in his hair and juicy red stains like blobs of blood soaking through his clothing. Getting frantic, getting hooked, getting tangled.

Bang! The door again. If she doesn't knock it off its hinges it'll be a living miracle. Josh lying doggo.

"George!"

Talk about temper. Who'd be a cat and live with an old woman?

"I'm not buying liver, George, to feed filthy blowflies."

Something's wrong, isn't it? More than there ought to be. Josh asking himself the question even while he listened. She's so mad with everything, so mad she's almost sobbing. Those kids all around. Those kids who hate my guts and love her. They'll hear. Pull your horns in, Aunt Clara, or it's something else I'll be blamed for.

"Even a cat won't answer ..."

Gone again. Still talking, talking until the depths of the house turned her voice into silence. Knocking on his door probably. Knocking there, calling, no answer coming back. A silent room ignoring her.

What'll she be saying? "Answer me, Josh." Not a sound from inside, not even breathing. Turning on the doorknob, door not yielding.

Don't weaken, Josh; it's still the same principle. She's the one who sent you packing. She's the one who pushed you into trouble. Her fault, Josh, not yours.

But I'm crying for her, honest.

Those kids at the bottom of the garden. Are they there? Were they ever there? Could they have passed it over and not said something to each other? No buzz of voices, nothing like a whisper, and the fence is close enough, by crikey. But hearing her perform like a maniac, wouldn't they have headed for home out of sheer embarrassment? The way you'll have to go now, Josh, no question about it. Out of sheer embarrassment? Something added to the day. Something not expected.

Mum, that rolling wheel. Doesn't it ever come to a hill it can't climb?

Blackbirds in the raspberries, used to him now, methodically stealing. Mosquitoes under the leaves whining at his ears, massing round his ankles, pestering him. A young magpie raucous for his mother somewhere handy. Spiders in the canes. Ants on the ground. It's a long way to Melbourne, Josh; still a hundred miles.

Hours and hours of daylight left in the sky. Trying to get more comfortable without disturbing anything, trying to swat mosquitoes without slapping loudly.

Josh, this is crazy.

Ryan Creek goes about its business, whatever its business may be. Josh Plowman in the raspberries, squirming and wriggling and itching.

Look at yourself as others might see you.

Is it manly?

Aunt Clara at your door, knocking. You in the raspberries, scratching. Mum at home sweetly ignorant imagining your simple enjoyments. Betsy close enough to shout at but as distant as distant can be.

Letter to Betsy.

Dear Betsy,

If I write to you will you write back because I know we're never going to get round to talking? I'm going, Betsy, because I can't show my face on the street any more. Why did you all have it in for me? Not because of my cousins, surely? Were you jealous or something because Aunt Clara was my auntie? And one thing led to another? Because you're here all the time doing things for her and I come barging in to get special treatment? Like my cousins before me? Strike me, it's a thought, isn't it? Like them all before me? Because I keep on thinking they're crummy, but not half as crummy as I keep on hearing. Did you want Aunt Clara for yourselves or something? You're welcome, you know, you can have her. Has she promised to leave you her money? Strike me, the plot thickens. Is she giving it to the town, her house and everything? It's like a museum already. Is that why everybody does things for nothing? A secret agreement, all the town in it, but the family not knowing? Well, good luck to you, Betsy. If that's what it is, good luck to you all with knobs on. That'll put a few noses out of joint round the family and send Mum off into hysterics. You'll hear her laughing from here. Where were we, dear Betsy? I reckon you're terrific though you've done nothing to make me think it. You've never said a nice word, never looked at me kindly, and I don't take any notice of stupid Rex and his urging. He was sniffing for trouble so he could stir it up with Harry. If I had any brains I'd hate you. I don't hate you, Betsy. I'd like to hold you by the hand and go running over mountains. But I'll not be doing it, ever. And I'll never write this letter and you'll never answer.

Letter to Laura.

Dear Laura,

I know you wrote your poem even though you tell lots of whoppers. I know why you jumped off the bridge, to prove you could really do something and not be robbed of the achievement. That was very brave of you but it wasn't fair to shift the blame because you were mad with Josh Plowman. Why did you say you didn't have a mother? What a stupid way to stop me. If I'd gone to your place for pancakes I'd have found out immediately. I'll go on trying to understand, Laura, but I reckon I'll be trying for ages. People are different, that's what they're always telling me, but you're the most different ever. I could write a book about you, Laura. You're a mystery.

Letter to Harry.

> *Dear Harry,*
> *Blurts!*

Letter to Bill.
> *Dear Bill,*
> *One of these days I could be bigger than you. If so, you'd*
> *better find a rabbit hole, mate, and crawl down it.*

Letter to Sonny.

> *Dear Sonny,*
> *I know why Rex was as sick as a dog on Sunday. He's*
> *been smoking cigarettes. Tell him you don't want his lousy*
> *money, tell him you want cigarettes for yourself, or else*
> *you'll be seeing his mother. Light 'em up, kid, suck deep,*
> *enjoy yourself, it's later than you think.*

Josh manfully chewing cheese of the sharpest disposition, stoking up on protein, itching and scratching, and swatting at mosquitoes.

34

Josh suddenly under pressure, almost choking on his protein. Sounds of sharp upheaval in the homestead. A wail as from a great-aunt deprived unexpectedly of a nephew. Doors banging.

"Josh! Josh!" A cry from the High Street that must have frightened the birds in the cemetery pine-trees.

Josh chewing on his cheese frantically to dispose of it.

More doors banging. Maybe the same ones still swinging. Shoes clattering on floorboards and bluestone.

"Josh!" A shout from the veranda that started dogs barking on the hillside.

Josh spitting out cheese he couldn't swallow and narrowly arresting the impulse to leap up and run for it. She's read it, she's read it, sprung the lock and read it hours before you reckoned.

"Josh, come back, come back this instant!"

Aunt Clara talking to herself nineteen to the dozen, into the house again like a whirlwind.

Josh crawling furiously down the garden as far as the fence would permit him. Fence like the Great Wall of China. Only paling fence in the district that wasn't falling over.

Aunt Clara out in the High Street yelling for the neighbours, Josh crawling along the fence-line as fast as hands and knees could carry him, battering through the undergrowth trying not to panic, looking for a gap in the palings wide enough to squeeze through.

Head for the wide blue yonder before she calls the army. While they're gathering in the High Street they'll not be watching out the back way. Blocked by gooseberry bushes sprouting thorns like needles, gooseberry bushes and pear-trees in a ferocious tangle. Up the fence and over it with a burst of animal vigour, sprawling yards into the open. Empty paddocks against him and the railway station below them with the creek in the gully. No one in the way, Josh. All clear for the sprint to freedom like your mother was a greyhound. No kids waiting to get you. No troopers lined up with cannon. Two cows only, chained to their orbits. Vaulting into the paddocks running like crazy, bundle in his raincoat streaming out behind him, ruts as rough as gutters, scared he'd twist an ankle, cow dung everywhere not even dodging it. One more fence to hurdle. Somehow scrambling over it. Crashing into the gully short of the railway boundary, reeling down the bank into the scrub by the water, sliding to his knees, sinking to his elbows, groaning into the earth, dazed from wild exertion. Dazed and groaning and afraid he might vomit.

Josh, have you done it?

Groping through his pockets for apples and carrots and his stub of lead pencil. Closing a hand over his notebook of poetry. Feeling his bundle of clothing still unbroken. You've got here, Josh, and not lost anything. Got here without falling over. Got here with no one pounding down behind you or yelling that they've seen you. Unbelievable. A little bit of panic but not enough to wreck it. You're out of that garden. Where you can't hear her talking, where she can't upset you, and won't tumble over you.

Josh vomiting.

35

Harry could have been there for minutes or might have just arrived. Josh looking up out of his sickness and there was Harry in his cricket clothes.

"Take your time, Joshua. We've got all day, thanks to your generosity."

Josh dropping his chin to his chest, slumping with a hand to the side, his world falling apart with sighs that happened out loud.

"I told them you'd show yourself when you got back your nerve. Too thick-skinned to lie low for a day. All we had to do was hang around."

Josh pushing clear of the ground he had fouled, hating Harry for being there to see.

"But what's the hurry down the hill, kid? Auntie finally decided she's stood all she can stand? Aiming to tan your hide?"

Josh saying nothing. His voice would have sobbed just then if he had spoken a word.

"Do you know what we're suggesting for you? We're suggesting you leave town. We're suggesting you get homesick real soon and nag your auntie to let you go. We don't go for kids like you. You're the daddy of them all right; you've got style all your own. A whole heap of fellows today, all dressed up for a game, hordes coming to watch them play. You know how far some of those Croxley kids had to come? We haven't got buses round the next corner like you kids in town. You know they've got to hang round here till eight o'clock tonight waiting for the train?"

Josh levelling out inside, very low, very flat, wondering whether it was worth the candle even to try. "I'm sick of the sound of your crummy cricket match. Look, did you ever really want to play? Was I supposed to turn up or wasn't I? Who told me to stay home? Who threatened to get me if I showed?"

"That doesn't cut any ice any more. You know everything changed."

"Nothing changed. If I played I got beaten up. If I didn't play I got beaten up. You tell me how it changed. No, don't tell me. Keeping up with you kids is something I can't do. You want me to leave town so I leave town. Will that do? Will that make it square? Will I go now?"

"Don't be a clown."

Josh dragging himself to his feet feeling like death warmed up, pulling his bundle off the ground and slinging it from his shoulder. "I'm going. I'm ready, see. Just get me out so Aunt Clara doesn't know."

Josh pushing off along the creek trying to step round Harry but meeting Harry's hand, a handful of shirt almost stretching him to his toes.

"You reckon on running away?"

"If you like."

"That's what you were doing racing down the hill? Already on your way?"

"That's what I was doing."

"That's why your auntie was yelling her head off?"

"That's why."

"Isn't there any end with you? How can any one kid be so low? How low do you reckon you can get?"

"Lower yet. When I hit the bottom you can move over to make

room. Take your hand off my shirt."

Harry screwing it violently and pushing him away.

Josh spinning for yards onto his back in the scrub, branches cracking under him, twigs spiking him, breathless from the shock of it, but past it all now, past everything, lying there enduring his indignity. "If you're trying for a fight, Harry, I can't care. I keep telling you kids I've not done anything. I keep telling you. All I want to do is go."

"That's what we want, Joshua, real bad, but not so you leave your auntie tearing her hair. That wasn't the idea. She's kind of special round here."

"You mean for sneering at?"

Harry making two savage paces, but pulling up sharply. "You're begging for it!"

"Go ahead. You're safe, I won't hit back."

Harry looking as Bill had looked in the High Street a few hours ago, but holding himself in check almost with his own hands, his voice thin with strain. "No one sneers at her. I don't care what you heard or thought you heard, no one was sneering at *her*."

"Tell it to the marines. I've got ears. I'm not stupid."

Harry with his features set fighting a battle of some kind, Josh not even worrying what it was about, not caring, unsteadily finding his feet again expecting to be flattened.

Harry saying, "She's been hearing it all."

"If that's the way you want it, sure. I've been running to her all the time. Now can I go?"

"You're asking for it! Oh, you're sitting up and begging for it. ..."

"I told you, go ahead. I don't care."

"You'll care if I do."

"I won't."

Harry's clenched fists dropping away. "I don't know, I don't know." Shaking his head. "I don't know what a bloke can do with you. You say you don't care and I know you don't. You don't care. ..."

"That's right. Now can I get out of town?"

"You've left her a note or something?"

"That's what I did."

"Telling her you were running away?"

"If that's the way you want it."

"It's got nothing to do with the *way I want it*!"

"If I told you the truth you wouldn't believe. You're too used to lies."

Harry looking almost desperate, like a grown-up man defeated by a small boy. "So you left her screaming her head off?"

"That's right."

"I'm taking you back to her."

"No, you're not. I'm only getting in the way. Me and this town and everyone in it; we're incompatible. Including her. Why she ever asked me to come I'll never know."

"Wasn't the asking the other way around?"

"Whatever you say. You had it all worked out between you before I got here. Now can I go? I want to breathe some fresh air."

Harry suddenly swinging with a flat hand catching Josh below the ear knocking him down. Josh sitting at Harry's feet with a hand to his neck, dazed.

"That's for her! What have I got to lose? Get up." Josh getting up obediently, not knowing what else to do, Harry instantly slapping him again, dropping him to his knees.

"And that's for the three of us who used to go to high school from here. I guess we'll not be going any more."

Josh moaning. "What's that got to do with me? What else am I getting blamed for?"

"Get up."

Harry wrenching him to his feet by the arm and punching him under the ribs, Josh falling like someone at prayer.

"That's for beating up a little kid, for trying to stop him from telling us what he saw, like any little kid would do. You're getting off lightly. Better from me than from his father. Up again. Up again."

Josh clinging to Harry's legs but feeling the drive of a knee against his collar-bone and the shock of cold water, sprawling in the creek running a foot deep, not knowing how he got there.

"And that's for Laura. Getting off *extra* lightly. I've been thinking of chucking you off the bridge. That's what I've been thinking of. But you're not worth the risk of murder."

Josh in a fog groping to the bank, clinging there to reeds.

"If you think I feel good for punching up a Plowman, that's what I hate you for."

Harry reaching for Josh's wrist and dragging him onto dry land. "Pull yourself together. I'm taking you back to her. I'll tell her I did it and I'll tell her why. Then what she does about it is up to her."

Josh drawing from his hip pocket his book of poems, binding broken, ink all running, pages all wet, looking up at Harry and crying.

"Well, I'll be jiggered." Harry staring down. "He's human. He can be hurt. He can cry for something other than a rabbit."

Josh in blinding fury wheeling his body on the ground and lashing out with both feet for Harry. Harry not there. Harry not waiting to be kicked or crippled. Two knees with all Harry's weight behind them falling on Josh, crushing him. Josh pinned on his chest in seconds, struggling uselessly, his right arm wrenched up behind him, his book being forced from his fingers.

"What is it? Your confessions? If you don't want it torn let go of it."

"Don't tear it. ..."

"I won't, if you let go of it."

"Don't *tear* it!"

A wrench on his right arm, tearing into his shoulders, and his book was gone and Harry was gone, his weight suddenly lifting.

"All right, now be good and come quietly. When we get you home you can have it back again."

Josh lying on his face, shaking. "You've torn it."

"I told you to let go of it."

"You've torn it. ... Even if you hate me. ..."

"Oh, turn it up. Do you think you're Shakespeare? Don't carry on like a baby. At least you had arrogance, Joshua; it gave you some style."

"I've been writing them since I was little."

"Too long. They've given you delusions of grandeur. You can dry 'em and stick 'em together again for your grandchildren. If Laura had broken her neck we wouldn't have been *sticking* her together again." Harry's fingers taking a rough bite on Josh's shirt and dragging him to his knees, then spinning him somehow and sitting him. "A beautiful sight you look. She'll think you've been hit by a truck."

Josh after a while realizing that a silence was growing where everything had been a noise, finding Harry with his eyes, Harry all blurred because everything was blurred, Harry looking odd because everything was odd.

"Come on, Josh, up you get."

Josh. From Harry?

A hand coming down taking him, not seizing him. "Let's go home to your auntie."

Josh rising.

Great-grandfather, I'm glad you can't see me.

Josh walking behind Harry.

Aunt Clara, I'm sorry I come back to you not like Josh Plowman, but like the kids I take home to my mother, kids we're sorry for because they don't fit in with others.

Harry holding his arms like a barrier, Josh blundering into the back of him, not seeing. Harry saying quietly, "Don't panic. Stick behind me. I'll get you through it. Show a bit of spirit."

A group of boys in white coming down from the footbridge by the railway station, vaulting from it or sliding from it or dropping from it into the gully, more than half of them strangers, some of them looking as big as Bill and as strong as Harry, a couple of them calling, "Is that him? Have you got him?"

"I won't let them hurt you."

That's fine, Harry. You and what army?

Harry walking on towards them, Josh stumbling after him.

Confrontation.

Harry with his arms out, again like a barrier, Josh behind it, heaven alone knew how many kids in front of it, maybe thirty.

"It's him, isn't it?"

Harry saying. "He's had his share. No more. He's had enough."

"You might have had your share, Harry, we haven't had ours."

"You've had yours, too. I've squared for the lot of us."

"You must be kidding."

"I'm not kidding. Fair's fair. He's paid for everything."

Josh knew that Harry wouldn't be stopping them. With all the will in the world he'd never be stopping them. Josh looking for faces he'd seen at Sunday-school. None of them friendly.

"Come on, Harry, give over. Let's at him."

"He's paid up for Ryan Creek and he's paid up for Croxley. And he's paid up for everything else he's been doing. *Rex*!" Harry suddenly shouting. "Get Bill! Bring him running!"

Josh couldn't see Rex anywhere. Rex keeping tags? Was it Rex who had spotted him racing to the gully?

"What do you want Bill for?"

"What do you reckon?"

"Look, Harry, you couldn't be sticking up for this character. You couldn't."

"That's what I'm doing. He's had his share I tell you."

"Aw, Harry."

"You couldn't."

"Harry, don't push us."

"I'm not pushing. I'm telling. If he gets hit again you'll hurt him."

"Who's going to hit him?"

"Yeh, who said hitting?"

"You can't fight all of us, Harry, and we're going to have him."

Kids coming, five or six of them together suddenly whooping, as many and more behind them, Josh glimpsing his book flying in pieces from somewhere out of Harry, Harry slinging punches but kids all over him, trampling on pages and trampling on bodies, Josh on the ground half-suffocated, kicking and writhing and then being frog-marched, being rushed into nowhere, great long strides, each as if falling from a precipice, kids all round him shoving and yelling, running into nowhere, driving him until his senses were reeling. Mum, they'll kill me, I can't keep going. Blundering into scrub, blundering through bushes, whipped by foliage, great long strides toppling. Someone screaming, "There are traps. Be careful." His shirt tearing up the back like paper, kids still pushing him keeping him running, floundering in the middle of them sprawling, kids all over him ripping his clothes off him. Harry, where are you, what are they doing to me? Bill, aren't you coming ever? A terrible rumpus, kids shouting and shrieking as if fights were happening at the fringes but still they had him, held by his extremities, kids carrying him by the corners like a sack of pumpkins, bouncing him and wrenching him as if they each wanted a piece of him, kids slipping and slithering and swinging him chanting, flying wildly through the air, water crashing all around him.

Josh trying to find a bottom to stand on, nothing to hang to, nothing to put his feet on, nothing but water and darkness and no breath to breathe with.

Josh drowning.

36

This is unexpected. I mean, who would have thought it? You come to Aunt Clara's after putting it off for a lifetime and end up dying. Tuesday is doomsday. End up getting murdered, maybe. Depends how they'll look at it. Lynched by public opinion. What a bally silly thing to happen. They might as well have hung you from the trestles and made a proper job of it. Dying, Great-grandfather, with your bridge looming over me, not that that's helping and not that it's hurting. Maybe hanging would have been more painfuL They always say drowning's pleasant, comparatively speaking, and there's something to it. Maybe I confirm it. But it's a cow, isn't it? Wednesday for burying.

Letter to Mum and Dad and Caroline.

Dear Mum and Dad and Caroline,
  It's been nice knowing you.

Josh gulping air as well as water. Someone yelling, "Keep your head up, can't you!" Another body wallowing alongside him, all legs and hands and splashes, propping him up by an armpit and blowing like a porpoise. Josh making strange noises and thinking of a postscript to Mum and Dad's letter, sighting an unfamiliar face through oceans of water.

"Are you all right now?" The boy still yelling.

Josh spluttering.

The boy taking his support away, Josh sinking feet-first down-wards, the boy dragging him up again.

"Can't you swim?"

Josh spluttering.

The boy shrieking shorewards. "What did I tell you? He can't swim. We coulda drowned him."

Kids rushing into the water, some running, some diving, Josh seeing them vaguely like something that had happened years ago or in a dream half-remembered.

PS. to Mum and Dad and Caroline.

Be seeing you sooner than expected.

"Hold on, matey. Keep your head up, won't you?"

Kids still coming, pouring in from the edges, prancing out like ponies or plunging into the shallows. Turning it into a ceremony. Attendance compulsory. Last in a lemon. They'll drown you yet, Josh, from sheer weight of numbers. Floating him back to shore like a royal progress, gravely, tenderly, all like loving brothers. Profoundly bewildering.

"Are you all right, fella? We've got y' safe. You're not drownin'."

"We didn't wish you no real harm, you know that, don't you?"

"Gee, matey, you should've told us. You should have yelled blue murder. Gee, matey, we might have drowned you. Why didn't you tell us you weren't a swimmer?"

"Yeh, duckin's constitutional."

"*Tra—ditional*, nitwit."

"Give him air there. Don't crowd him."

"Do you want pumping out, fella?"

"Cor, he's a horrible colour."

"Roll him over. You go, Joe, you're the expert at it."

Josh waving weakly to be left to recover. Moaning. "No, no. Don't resuscitate me. I couldn't stand it."

Kids stretching him along the bank, putting his head down gently.

"You sure you don't want pumpin'?"

"No pumping. Please, no pumping."

"Y'ought to pump him, Joe, don't you reckon?"

"Leave him a minute. See what he looks like."

"Looks like he's dyin'."

"Cor, ain't he skinny?"

"Don't they feed you, matey?"

"Poor skinny fella. Looks real underprivileged, don't he? Poor little city kid livin' in an alley. Lift his head up, Davey. Don't leave him in a puddle."

"Gee, we're sorry, matey. We didn't know you were a sickie or anything. They didn't tell us."

"Fetch his pants, Ossie. Poor kid lyin' here naked. It ain't decent. Specially bein' so skinny."

Josh feeling it might be proper to die immediately.

"You Ryan Creek kids. Are you cracked or something? Look at him. You said he'd been raising Cain and Abel. He couldn't have held the bat up, poor fella. Hit him with the ball and we woulda killed him."

"Let's duck 'em, I say. Let's give 'em their own medicine."

"Yeh, let's get 'em, Croxley. That's why there wasn't no cricket."

"Scared of gettin' towelled. Scared of losin'. Blamin' it on this poor fella."

"Chuck 'em in the river! At 'em, Croxley!"

Uproar. Instant chaos. Josh left to suffer without their ministrations, in dire danger of being kicked senseless, trying to crawl for safety through a milling mob of cricketers. Fists flying everywhere. Kids running riot in astonishing numbers, maybe he was seeing double, kids pouring down the back road from the High Street, leaping off their bicycles and two-wheeled scooters, wheels in the air spinning, kids racing along the track below the railway embankment yelling like Indians and rushing into it, car brakes squealing, girls and grown-ups and shrilling women. Josh lying prostrate on his belly in the open, bottom uppermost, wailing for a bit of privacy. Fights raging yards out in the water, kids swimming for the trestles, pursuers after them, a man in umpire's clothing cracking heads together and yelling madly for order, schoolmaster Cotton wading in from another direction looking like Samson and sending kids flying, standing over Josh a leg to each side of him, dropping his black silk coat to cover him. Standing up there above him shouting hoarsely, "Stop it. Stop it. Stop it. Stop it." Wasting his energy and finishing up with words that sounded strongly like swearing, Josh making a vague note of them for future investigation. A hand touching him, Josh turning his head and there was Aunt Clara kneeling at his shoulder. Her hand caressing his arm and reaching to his fingers, lifting them and kissing them.

Strike me, Aunt Clara, that's real nice of you, considering everything. Do you know what they're doing? *They're* ALL *fighting for me.*

Schoolmaster Cotton lifting him from the ground bodily, Aunt Clara arranging the coat to cover his embarrassment, Josh collapsing all ways simultaneously, no need to fight for survival any longer. Josh being carried. Beautiful security. Beautiful security.

Jammed into the back seat of the schoolmaster's Baby Austin, lolling, Aunt Clara squashing in to support him, Josh not seeing too well, not caring much for anything.

"To Dr. Robertson, if you don't mind, Mr. Cotton, straight to him."

The Austin climbing the hill, dozens of kids in muddy disorder, running, strung out behind it, not entirely pleased with themselves; that's what Aunt Clara was saying.

37

"Josh ... would you like to sit up now?"

What time was it? Felt like tomorrow.

Josh on his back blinking at the chandelier shivering, lights in the crystals, blues and reds and yellows in tiny tinkling flashes, curtains drawn wide, outside everything a kind of cobalt greyness. It wasn't a bad room, not really. Interesting. When you got used to it, the colours made a unity you'd always remember. Great-grandfather's bedroom. Exactly as he had left it, for a quarter of a century, except for stinking lavender. Great-grandfather still possessing it grandly.

"Aunt Clara, what time is it?"

"A little after eight, dear."

"What day is it?"

"Same as earlier."

"The day I died, Aunt Clara, almost. I was drowning."

"It has been an experience for all of us. Fortunately salutary."

"Aunt Clara, have you ever been drowning?"

"No, dear."

"I have. Gee, Aunt Clara. ..."

Tears, no stopping them. Tears shaking him and blinding him.

Aunt Clara stroking his brow, whispering, "They respect you now, Josh. All of them. The truth will out, you know. You've been what this town needed—a catharsis." Aunt Clara smiling.

"Remember you're a Plowman and he's watching."

Great-grandfather in his regalia presiding.

Josh sitting up, sniffing. Aunt Clara mopping his face with her apron and holding it in place for nose-blowing. Propping him up with pillows. Placing his tray in front of him.

"It looks nice, Aunt Clara. Smells good."

"You must be hungry, poor fellow."

"I won't be able to eat without washing."

"That sounds unduly fastidious. You were bathed at the doctor's. Don't you remember? Thoroughly. Hot water on tap. Very handy in an emergency."

"Am I injured or anything terrible?"

"You'll be up and around tomorrow. As bright as a button, I'm thinking. Hard as nails, was the doctor's opinion. I would not have believed it."

"Aunt Clara, what's a catharsis?"

"A clearing-out, my dear, of the digestive system. A purgation."

"Oh, Aunt Clara, what a horrible thing to call me."

"There's another meaning, but I like the one I've chosen. Now eat your dinner. It's much too good to be fed to the chickens. ... Harry is very troubled, Josh. Trying to find your poems. Trying to piece them together. Don't worry, he'll not be telling people what he's reading. Harry's very humble and feels wholly responsible—for vandalism, as he calls it—which he isn't. A fine boy is Harry and very clever, a boy who must not be wasted. I think you know that, don't you? Your conflict with him was a conflict of principles. Harry thought he was right, but Harry was lied to, he was not the liar. Do I need to go further?"

"You might need to, Aunt Clara. Harry told his share of them. He said you were poor and called me a sponger. That was Harry."

"Was it?"

"Yes, ma'am. How can I be the sponger? You're not paying for my education. But you're paying for his—aren't you? —and for Bill's and Betsy's I reckon, or they'd be out working for a living like the rest of them."

Aunt Clara frowning. "Do you realize what you've done? Put a particular kind of finger on Harry. You've not done it before with anyone. That's an important reason for having friends outside, new ones, and lots of them. Why put the finger on Harry, who least deserves it?"

"It's not for me to say, Aunt Clara. That's the way it strikes me. You've got to ask yourself the question, I reckon."

"I am disappointed in many, but not in Harry. You understand me?"

"Yes, Aunt Clara."

"Good. I don't want to labour it and I'd like it kept between us. ... What I do in this town with what little I have is my own business. There's been a very serious depression and you were lucky. It didn't hit the Plowmans as it hit many people. Harry's very sensitive; there have been tragedies in his family. I know you'll forgive the other young people—they've learnt their lesson—but you don't have to forgive Harry. That would be belittling him. Shake hands with him. Say nothing. And accept the gift he brings you. A new notebook for new poems. A very good one that he'll be working hard to pay for." Aunt Clara talking quickly as if subjecting him to pressure. "Josh, you know Harry's very fond of Betsy."

"Yes, Aunt Clara."

"I suppose if a lad of his age can love a girl, he loves her. You've impressed Betsy; perhaps you didn't guess it. Under that surface she's a shy little creature. Don't spoil it for Harry."

"Now wait a minute. ..."

"Will you do that for me?"

Josh's heart turning over. "I can't promise things like that, Aunt Clara."

"I'm hoping you will."

"Well I can't and I won't. Golly, Aunt Clara. … You're pushing me. One thing after the other; you're still pushing me. I'll not be promising that, ever, but there's something I wouldn't mind doing, just the same."

"What's that?"

"I'd like to start walking home tomorrow."

Aunt Clara's smile fading. "Josh. …" Sounding wounded and astonished.

"I mean it. I'm old enough. I'm strong enough. After today I can stand anything."

"Is your heart so hard? You couldn't do that to them."

"Nothing to do with a hard heart; nothing to do with it. I thought you'd know. It's this living in the sun. It's wearing me ragged."

"Josh, that's cruel."

"You can say that again, Aunt Clara, it's the right word for it."

"Oh, Josh, they expect you. … They're so sure of it. All sorts of plans they've been making—"

"Or you've been making for them?"

"That's unkind. Cricket again on Thursday, all the Croxley boys coming back to play. And Ballarat for the two of us tomorrow. And a picnic on Saturday in your honour. Everyone coming. It's their apology. You've got to let them make it. Josh, they're so looking forward to your company."

Aunt Clara taking dishes, leaving the room in a flutter, Josh looking up to Great-grandfather. We've heard all that before, sir, haven't we? Look where it got us. Too many loose ends already and the longer I stay the more there will be. It's not cut and run, sir, not exactly, but staying on till Monday? I reckon that'll kill me. They'll bury me, Great-grandfather, I know it. They'll be digging me a hole beside you.

Here lies Josh Plowman. Catharsis.

WEDNESDAY

Josh looking back to the bridge put there by Great-grandfather in 1882, looking back again and again, the least he could do while they stood to watch him go. Looking back and waving, picking different faces while faces could be seen, Aunt Clara with a table-cloth flapping it up and down as if saying here I am, here I am, Josh, come back, change your mind. Josh waving each time until she was gone from view.

Blue sky and yellow stubble, golden yellow plain, singing in the sun, kicking up his heels; brother, it can even rain.

Go away, crows. Find yourselves a body that's had its day. I'm walking mine to Melbourne town and living every mile.

Ivan Southall

Ivan Southall is one of Australia's best-known and prolific writers for children and young adults. Four of his novels won the Children's Book of the Year Award from the Children's Book Council of Australia: *Ash Road* in 1966, *To the Wild Sky* in 1968, *Bread and Honey* in 1971, and *Fly West* in 1976. His work has been translated into 23 languages.